TWO DOGS
AT THE
ONE DOG INN
AND OTHER STORIES

Also by David John Griffin

The Unusual Possession of Alastair Stubb (2015)
Infinite Rooms (2016)
Abbie and the Portal (2018)
Turquoise Traveller (2019)

TWO DOGS AT THE ONE DOG INN

and other stories

DAVID JOHN GRIFFIN

First published in Great Britain in 2017 by Urbane Publications Ltd
Suite 3, Brown Europe House, 33/34 Gleaming Wood Drive, Chatham, Kent ME5 8RZ

This edition published by David John Griffin

A CIP catalogue record for this book is available from the British Library.

ISBN 978-0-9930445-4-0

Cover design by David John Griffin
Text design & typeset by David John Griffin

Printed in Great Britain by Amazon Kindle Direct Publishing

To Susan, Lynn & Mum

"Science cannot solve the ultimate mystery of nature. And that is because, in the last analysis, we ourselves are a part of the mystery that we are trying to solve."

Max Planck

CONTENTS

Novella

TWO DOGS AT THE ONE DOG INN 1

Short stories

HENRIETTA 112
CLARA SEAWARD'S PAINTINGS 116
RETURN TO THE SEA 125
A CROUCHING MAN 135
THE CONVERSION OF RUSCOE ROBINSON 139
THE HIDDEN LIBRARIES OF
DOCTOR DANCER 166
MOBILE 173
THE ULTIMATE SECRET 192
ANGELINE 201
THE BENEFACTOR AND THE GHOST 210
DAISY 8112 217
THE EXTRAORDINARY TALE OF KASSARA 218

TWO DOGS AT THE ONE DOG INN

Email From: Audrey Ackerman 29 May 2013 14:11
To: Stella Bridgeport Insults

Dear Stella, or should we just forget the "dear"? I'm still steaming. How dare you say I was hysterical. And even if I was, I had a right to be, as I tried to explain. During my phone call late this morning while still shaking from my crazy experiences, I expected some sympathy but instead all I got were insults to my intelligence. And to the state of my mind (which is fine, thank you very much). I thought you of all people would understand.

Quite frankly, I can't handle it any more. You didn't want to know, didn't even offer any help. Please don't expect me back at the Centre ever again. I've loved working for The Animal Welfare Union but enough is enough. So consider this email my official resignation. There are a few personal items to collect; I'll pick them up next week, after these dreadful incidents are less of a burden. And don't phone me. After your reactions this morning I don't want to talk to you again, sorry.
Audrey

•

Email From: Stella Bridgeport 29 May 2013 15:34
To: Audrey Ackerman Re: Insults

Dear Audrey, didn't intend insulting you this morning. Was trying my best to "snap you out of it". You were in quite a state. And to be honest, I couldn't get the gist of what you told me, for the most part. Something about dogs with eyes at The One Dog Inn? All dogs have eyes, don't they. You were crying so hard and talking so fast I didn't know what you were saying. Heard you mention a broken ankle. At least you haven't broken your ankle, got that much. Think I understood about the dogs escaping but that's about it. Remember me suggesting I come over to talk? With Robert as well, if you wanted? Perhaps not, you were screaming down the phone at the time. But doesn't matter. Obviously you've been deeply upset. I just couldn't (and still don't) grasp the reasons, that's all.

Anyway, that aside, please reconsider your decision. You so love the animals and you're one of our most popular volunteers, you really are. That's why so many people ask for you. And praise you. I will understand if you'd like to take a couple of weeks off. Get yourself relaxed and sorted. Then we can both start on the same foot again. What do you think? Take your time and let me know tomorrow. And if you feel up to it, more info concerning escaped dogs please? Asking a lot as you're upset. But don't want them roaming loose, agreed? Won't phone as requested but you can phone me if you like. Kind regards, Stella

•

Email From: Audrey Ackerman 29 May 2013 16:13
To: Stella Bridgeport Re: Insults

Dear Stella, alright, I did talk too fast, but was (still am) frightened. And confused, now I've started reading files from the memory stick. (Dennis transferred them to the iPad for me). This whole thing is either an elaborate hoax – a trick I unwittingly stumbled upon – or a waking nightmare. Whichever it is, I'm still upset by the way you responded. We're good friends after all these years, surely, and I don't expect to be spoken to like that by a friend. Perhaps I'll reconsider about leaving though. Give me a few days or more to calm myself and get in gear again then I'll get back to you with a decision. In the meantime, an apology wouldn't go amiss. There's no need for me to phone you either – in fact, I'd rather not for the while, but don't mind if we continue communicating via emails.

As for the two dogs, they're still within The One Dog Inn as far as I'm aware. The first dog, secured by a leash in the courtyard; the vanishing second one, still running free in the building, I suppose. All I can think is the staff will catch it when they've woken up (if they haven't already). These animals can't be my responsibility anymore. And even if they were, I couldn't bring myself to go anywhere near the poor creatures, especially the male which is so distressing to look at with those eyes the way they are, as I explained before. It's just not natural. I know I won't sleep tonight, my mind keeps on going back to them. Do hope I'm not developing an obsessive compulsive disorder or whatever. This whole episode has put my head in a spin. In fact, I'm still feeling physically sick. Bye.

•

Email From: Stella Bridgeport 29 May 2013 18:07
To: Audrey Ackerman Re: Insults

Dear Audrey, thanks for letting me know about those dogs. Got to dash now. Robert's taking me to see that play, the one in Brabbington village hall tonight? Welcome to come with us. Going to be fun. It'll help ease your worries. The play starts at 7.30. Let me know and if you'd like to join us we'll pick you up at 7. Please try to make it. And of course we are friends, and I apologize. Didn't mean to upset you.

It's a good idea for you to relax and unwind over the next couple of days. Hopefully you'll be able to see with a fresh perspective. As for developing a disorder, no you're not. Whatever upsets you had have simply made an impact on your temperament. This won't be permanent, I'm certain.

I'm getting more muddled though, I must mention. Now you've been talking about a memory stick. I don't recall you mentioning a memory stick this morning. Audrey, why not take me through the whole sequence of events. Step by step, in writing. Then not only will it aid in emptying your mind of whatever happened, once you've committed it to paper (or email – you know what I mean) then I can piece it together better and try my best to help. OK, must go. Don't forget to message me about the play as soon as. Regards from Stella

•

Email From: Audrey Ackerman 29 May 2013 18:19
To: Stella Bridgeport Re: Insults

Stella, count me out for the play but thanks for thinking of me. I hope you and Robert have an enjoyable evening.

I mentioned the memory stick this morning, I'm sure I did — dug up by the grey dog. Suddenly realized how strange this is sounding; you surely must think I've lost a marble or two. Perhaps I have…

Thank you for your apology. But now I see you didn't need to apologize – my fault, I threw all of this over the phone. In a way I shouldn't have got you involved and lumbered you with my problems. It's like I've entered a bad dream that I can't escape from. Regards, Audrey

P.S I'll have a hot soak tonight, a lay-in tomorrow and see if I'm in a better state to put it in writing, like you suggest; aim to email later in the afternoon. Hopefully explaining will help erase these frightening memories, lay them to rest somehow.

•

Email From: Audrey Ackerman 30 May 2013 16:15
To: Stella Bridgeport Tired + the play

I've read more from the memory stick. This weird stuff is down to the author of the files, I'm certain – a Mr. Gideon Hadley who claims to be a science fiction writer. I've never heard of him; not that I read those sorts of books, don't know about you. I've been trying to find out if he has any connection to television or film, you know, special effects and the like. That's what it's all about, The One Dog Inn is a filmset for a science fiction story, with skilfully made props and the staff made-up actors. It has to be that.

Feeling tired, Stella, I can't keep my eyes open. And this is after a sleep-in this morning. Don't know what's wrong, I'm usually full of life, aren't I. Got to have a nap now so I'll email tomorrow. Regards, Audrey

P.S I hope you and Robert had a lovely time at the play last night. Did you catch Cynthia there? I forgot to say: bumped into her last week and she asked after you. I don't know why I assumed she was going but she might have done.

•

Email From: Stella Bridgeport 31 May 2013 08:35
To: Audrey Ackerman Re: Tired + the play

Dear Audrey, sorry didn't get back to you yesterday, the Centre went manic. Frederick the basset was middle of an argument between the Riddle's and Carpenter's. I thought Desmond Carpenter finally agreed to let the Riddle family have him. Seems not. Suzie (the vet, not the handler) had a double shift. Bill came down with a stomach bug. He did look ill, drawn and white. Stubborn about leaving. I told him go, no use to anyone in his state.

A few excitements after, though won't bother you with them now. Enough to say the afternoon ended pretty well in the end.

Brabbington village hall is wonderful, isn't it? I'd forgotten what a terrific venue it is, those old beams spanning the massive barn areas. The renovation is superb. A nice touch for the audience sitting on bales of hay. Glad for the cotton covers. And the play was so funny! You should have come, would have loved it. Remember Percival, Edith's son? He stole the show, really he did. We almost rolled in the aisles, we were laughing so much! Has a real talent – should be professional. Didn't see Cynthia there. Thought I caught sight of her across the crowded bar in the interval but it was someone else (who could have been a long-lost sister). Never mind, I'll phone this evening to say hello. Not sure how we lost contact but you know the way it goes.

Hope you had a refreshing nap, as well as a quality night's sleep. I'm positive it's done you the world of good.

Still not totally getting this memory stick thing. Though files on it were written by a science fiction writer called Gideon Hadley, yes? Was he there when you attended to the dogs? Oh, Robert's beeping – car's here. Bye for now. (Do look after yourself). Best regards, Stella

•

Email From: Audrey Ackerman 31 May 2013 17:46
To: Stella Bridgeport Appointments

Stella, I forgot my two appointments yesterday, and what about Mr. Blakewood and his wolfhound today? He must be furious I let him down. But I can't bring myself to leave the house yet, sorry.

Glad you had a good time at the play in the barn. And I feel a little bit better, thanks, just worried about my visits.

I'll start writing what happened with regards to The One Dog Inn next email, if that's alright. I'll feel more up to it later today. Although do put my mind at rest with regards to the appointments, thanks. Regards, Audrey

•

Email From: Stella Bridgeport 31 May 2013 20:26
To: Audrey Ackerman Re: Appointments

All under control, Audrey. Don't worry. Two appointments yesterday were sorted. The Jack Russell owner postponed. And Suzie kindly stepped in and saw Mrs. Feathers for you (the lady with five cats, one of them with the eye infection). Did contact Mr. Blakewood but message unanswered. Try again tomorrow to arrange another time. Bound to accept (I'll say you weren't well). No need for fretting, OK? I'll look at your bookings for next week. Either they can be rescheduled, or Hazel and Suzie will stand in for you, if not busy those times. They really won't mind.

Back to this One Dog Inn business. I'll leave it to you when you want to tell me, as quickly as you like or in your own casual time. Next email or just when you're ready.

Last thing: Robert said if you need any help, shopping, for instance, just give the word and he'll get that done. Bye for now, running away from the computer to watch my drama. Second part tonight. Can't miss it, getting quite gripping! Kind Regards, Stella

•

Email From: Audrey Ackerman 01 June 2013 13:45
To: Stella Bridgeport Re: Appointments

Thank you, Stella, that's a small weight off my mind. Suzie and Hazel are stars, aren't they. And so is Robert – please tell him how kind he is to offer but I'm alright for food for a few days, weeks even. (I tend to overstock, been like that for ages; walk-in larder shelves always groaning with the weight of tin cans).

I made a start writing late this morning, as I find it easier getting memories down on paper as a list. I'll type them and expand on the list points soon. A fair bit to tell so I'll send it in chunks. And please try to understand, as unreal as it'll be when you read the emails, you have to believe me that it all happened. Kind regards, Audrey

•

Email From: Audrey Ackerman 01 June 2013 22:15
To: Stella Bridgeport Two dogs at The One Dog Inn

Dear Stella, I'll start with events on Tuesday. As requested, I drove to Cabbit's Farm (in Dronewich) late afternoon, to meet Eddie the farmer. By the way, his full name is Eddie Winslow, if you'd like to amend the file. (Cabbit was his mother's maiden name). You know I'm a stickler for detail. And because of that too, I won't worry about giving every scrap of information I can remember. As you said earlier, once I've put everything down as words, it'll help clear it out of my head.

The first incident disturbing my normally mellow self occurred while I was driving to reach the farm. From the main road there was a clear metal sign pointing to the start of a track so I naturally assumed that was the way. It began alright, enough room for two cars to pass, and the earth – or I should say, mud – had gravel over it. But further on, the track narrowed to a single car width, ugly bushes each side, and it had ruts and holes filled with water. I was not best pleased, though can't blame anyone but myself; I found out later that if I'd used my satnav it would have taken me along a made-up road — the one I discovered once I'd reached the farm's double gates.

Before that, I need to tell you something I'm not certain you'd be interested in hearing. I'll mention it all the same: I think I need my ears syringed. While travelling along that rutted country track, with the engine labouring every time I got stuck in a muddy puddle, I could have sworn I heard a dog barking yet it was the quirkiest barks I've ever heard. The only way to explain: they were like barked vowels but high-pitched. Every time I stalled the engine or stopped pressing on the accelerator,

I couldn't hear it any more.

Now with blocked up ears playing tricks, and discovering a concrete road when reaching the farm, I was already in a grumpy mood. Anyway, after getting out of the car and unlatching one of the gates, I went in and past agricultural sheds before I noticed a man standing by a tractor. I called over to ask if he was Farmer Eddie. As he began to answer, there were more barks and dog squeals carried on a warm breeze from over the fields at the back, those animals distressed, their noises amplified and echoing through the open-ended metal buildings. These were actual dog barks this time (not the quirky vowel ones).

The man wasn't the farmer; he directed me round the corner of the stables to a farmhouse hidden behind one of the barns. I rang the bell, the door opened and I was let in.

Even as the farmer made his official complaint, the dogs were clearly heard again through the open windows of the kitchen, their barks travelling across the countryside from The One Dog Inn approximately half a mile away. Looking out and over to the south side of Wetstone Hill, there can be seen jagged tops of the inn's gothic towers poking up above the distant bushes and trees. He told me how his own dogs, as well as the sheep and horses, had been disturbed so often. I informed him that the noise problem was probably more of a council concern. He said he'd phoned them several times and the replies were always the same: they would be looking into the matter. Passing it off, he felt. That's when I phoned (on

Tuesday afternoon) and we discussed the next course of action, agreeing I contact the inn and make an appointment to visit them a.s.a.p. I told Farmer Eddie this, got a few more details for the report sheet (which I've still got, do let me know if you need it soon), said goodbye, went back to the car, and phoned the inn.

Here's the next incident: after the mobile rang for a while, it was answered by a woman speaking metallic-sounding words. Yes, I know, you'd say my ears again or something wrong with the mobile's speaker, and at the time I thought the same. It was odd, with extra oddness as I heard sounds of the dog barks travelling across the fields once more, as well as from over the phone from their origin somewhere in The One Dog Inn.

It was a strained conversation, I must say; at least from my side, speaking to this female with a synthetic voice. After I explained about the complaint, and asked if tomorrow – the Wednesday – would be alright, she kept on repeating, "Help me, help you," in that peculiar tone. I had the idea she must have been using a man-made voice box to speak with, after surgery to replace a damaged larynx perhaps. Finally ringing off, I still wasn't clear if she understood I would be visiting next day. And when I did visit, I found out the real reason for the robotic-sounding quality. The filmset idea makes even better sense, now I think back. I'll tell you more proceedings of Wednesday in the next email. You're not going to believe it but you must.

Right, I've just seen the time: it's getting closer to 11pm so leaving it there tonight; I'll carry on tomorrow. Goodnight Stella, and thank you again for bothering with this and listening/reading. Kind Regards, Audrey

•

Email From: Stella Bridgeport 02 June 2013 16:39
To: Audrey Ackerman Re: Two dogs at The One Dog Inn

Hello Audrey, sorry for the delay in replying. It was too late to email last night. As for today, Robert and I spend our Sunday mornings in bed reading the newspapers. This is the first opportunity I've had since finishing dinner.

I think you've cracked it. It's your ears. I mean to say, we think you've got an ear infection. I know you won't mind me suggesting this: it's given you a subtle fever. Well, that's what I think. Robert disagrees, telling me you can't get a fever from an infected ear. But at least we both agree an infection can affect the senses.

All these unusual things that happened were caused by the infection. It changed your hearing and sight. Once you've taken a course of antibiotics and had your ears syringed, you'll be fighting fit again. How's that for detective work! So forget all that filmset stuff, as well as those files. See the lot as pure 100% fiction. Too bizarre, without relevance to anything, stirring you up too much. Don't get confused by nonsense any more: throw the memory stick in the bin!

I hope that's cleared your mind and put everything to rest. Spend a week relaxing while you're taking antibiotics and after, back to your happy work— those budgies, cats and dogs need you! Kind regards, Stella

•

Email From: Audrey Ackerman 02 June 2013 17:03
To: Stella Bridgeport Re: Two dogs at The One Dog Inn

Stella, are you even reading what I wrote? Or do you read between the lines and make two plus two equal five? Most of my words evaporated, didn't they? I could write a tome, a manuscript an inch thick, and still you'd take on board what you want, just a picky, misunderstood distillation. There's the danger you'll start me off again, really. I'm so annoyed. Where did the ear infection business come from? There's a bit more wax in my ear canal than usual; you know, everyday normal wax, not infected, not affecting the mind or sight in any way although possibly affecting my hearing to a small degree.

Also I have to say, I am not happy you're discussing this with Robert. This is between you and me only. Or was…

Listen, I'm close to having enough, just can't deal with this anymore. There's no hope you'll ever understand. But then I don't understand either so the whole situation is just a meaningless horror. I shouldn't have bothered trying to explain. Don't email back, Stella, there's no point.

•

Email From: Stella Bridgeport 02 June 2013 19:49
To: Audrey Ackerman Re: Two dogs at One Dog Inn

Audrey, please, I'm trying to help in the only ways I know how. Wouldn't upset you on purpose. I'm at a loss what to say now. Getting more confused every email you send. But want to understand, really do. Didn't mean to offend again either, by talking with Robert. I assure you, won't mention anything more to him, OK? Carry on, give the next chapter of what happened. Not going to say I can solve anything but I'm here to listen. Promise me and not do anything silly. Best regards, Stella

•

Email From: Stella Bridgeport 03 June 2013 18:36
To: Audrey Ackerman Re: Two dogs at The One Dog Inn

Audrey, haven't heard back from you. Please tell me you're alright. From your worried friend, Stella

•

Email From: Audrey Ackerman 03 June 2013 20:54
To: Stella Bridgeport Re: Two dogs at One The Dog Inn

Hello Stella, I'm alright, I've cooled down again. I know you're only trying to help and as you mentioned, it's all too bizarre, really it is. You just have to keep on reading, that's all I'm asking – no judgements, suggestions or attempted reasoning needed. And though I think there's a rational explanation for what's going on, I'm still a bit delicate, emotionally-speaking, and so kindly request you avoid any theories about the state of my mind.

And before you enquire again, I'll tell you that there's no ear infection (I visited the nurse at the surgery today for syringing and she confirmed it). Also I must add I'm not on any medication; in fact no drugs of any sort, legal or otherwise (rarely take paracetamol even).

This next chapter – to call it that, although I'll underline none of it is fiction, just what I remember – hasn't been influenced by any of the author's files either. Yet the more I read, the more I feel I could find a rational explanation in those files as to what happened at the inn. I've a notion to email them to you a couple at a time, later on.

I arrived outside of the tall wrought iron gates of the inn at 9.30am; a mounted camera scanned my windscreen. The gates opened automatically and after driving in, I was presented with one of those red and white striped pole barriers across their private road. I pressed the intercom, set in a post, and heard that electronic voice speaking, the one I wrote about in the previous email, repeating the same thing as the day before, over and over: "Help me, help you". The barrier rose; I drove slowly along the road through the grounds.

Two acres of land surround the inn, with herringbone paved walkways winding over grassed banks, and lawns covered with trees, pergolas and arches. Also a delightful boating lake (I'll tell you more about that later; enough to say I saw what can be described as a truly beautiful sight there, floating on the water).

Before I carry on, did you know The One Dog Inn is meant to be haunted? (And I believe it). Not surprising, I guess, as the main part of it was built in the 17th century – making the inn over 350 years old – more than enough time for it to acquire its fair share of ghosts and spectres.

For interest, I copied & pasted an entry about the inn from Cyclowik. Perhaps I copied too much but still, it might aid you in getting more of an idea of the place for when you read later on about my visit. There's another reason too but I'll explain that after the article. So if you skip any, at least make sure to read the section marked "Haunting and other Phenomena".

*****

The One Dog Inn, Legatemead
From Cyclowik, your free online encyclopedia

The One Dog Inn is a historic coaching house located in the English town of Legatemead[1] in the southern county of Kantem[2]. It has been a Grade II listed building since 21 August 1952. This defines the building as "particularly important which holds more than special interest".[3] The One Dog Inn is owned by Judith Pinner & Derek Fileman, who bought it in May 1993.[4] The inn is particularly well-known for its curious arrays of bottles held in place on marble plinths, buried in walls and set in granite floor tiles all within the confines of the building's courtyard.

In late 1985, the exterior of the inn, along with its grounds and cobbled tracks, were used in the feature film Masks of Glass[5].

1 Location and Geography [edit]

The inn is located facing south, towards One Dog Lane, on the outskirts of the main town, and sits east of Priors Gift Path, and is 0.4 miles (0.6 km) from Dronewich. The inn is within in its own grounds, an area of approx. 1 hectare, overlooking the Ridgeback Downs with Hingeferry Forest Country Park to the back of it. To its right can be found the large areas of meadow known locally as Gone-But-Not-Forgotten[6]. The inn is 2.4 miles (3.8 km) south east of Cattlemote railway station and 1.3 miles (2.1 km) west of the ancient site of the unusually named Cloisters of the Attendant Gods,[7] described [by whom?] as the original site of a monastery housing a medieval order of monks. Close by are working farms known as Cabbit's Farm, Sarah Fym, and Bottle Lane Farm. The inn is 25.2 miles (40.5 km) north of the town of Soundwich. The nearest airport is close to Dovegate, 27.7 miles (44.5 km) south east of the inn. Stokesflown is 31 miles [49.8 km] away, on the Kantem coast.

2 History [edit]

The current building dates from 1656 and has 18th- and early 19th-century additions in the Tudor and Neo-Gothic styles. The cellars built in 1237 survive. Inner courtyard walls have been dated to the end of the 14th-century (but were possibly built earlier), those being the only surviving parts of a larger medieval thatched construction – made of wattle and daub – burnt to the ground by fire [citation needed]. The inner courtyard walls are also referred to as "The Womb" although there is no elucidation to be found as to why they were given this name.

2.1 Early years

It has been proposed by local historians that the original medieval thatched building, which stood for at least 100 years on the site before the majority of it was destroyed, had connections with Cloisters of the Attendant Gods[7]; and a medieval manuscript found amongst the monastery ruins in 1809 seemed to add corroboration to that theory. In the manuscript it is written there existed a connecting tunnel between these two places (although neither the tunnel nor its entrances were ever found).

At least 60 years after the destruction of the thatched building, work was started on the inn, constructed around the remaining stone and flint courtyard, and completed in 1561 during the early part of the reign of Queen Gloriana I. The inn opened its doors to travellers shortly after and quickly became a notable ale house, with its own brewery in the cellars, and charging 1s. per night for lodging. Any reason why the inn was named The One Dog Inn is still unknown to this day.

Between 1567 and 1581, many functions were organized by local dignitaries, such as the "Special Gentlemen Dinner",

"Mayor's Night and Day Celebrations" and the strangely titled "Hacking The Fat Mackerel Feast"[8]. The inn also functioned as a Centre for indoor markets of produce such as fish, cloth, beer and sometimes wine. One of the larger galleried rooms was used as a banqueting hall for visiting groups, there to hunt wildfowl in the nearby lake.

2.2 Later years

In the beginning part of the 18th century, The One Dog Inn became popular with sailors from Stokesflown and later acquired strong connections with an infamous gang of smugglers who used it in the 1730s and 1740s as one of their strongholds. Stokesflown was a thriving port during that period and much was smuggled away from the docks to safe houses such as The One Dog Inn, bounty hidden in the cellars. The gang soon gained an infamous reputation and became known by many names, including The Stone Wall Gang, The Secret Door Gang and The Red Bottlers.

There were rumours that the select group of smugglers used numerous secret tunnels (including one believed to have run from the cellars to the Cloisters of the Attendant Gods[7]), secret doors and even a few revolving cupboards for making a quick getaway.[9] Residents of Legatemead remembered the smugglers as: "Nothing but proudness, insolence and sneers all the while, confidently dominating the inn, taking control of seats at the windows to smoke clay pipes, with loaded pistols on tables before them."

In the 1770s, additions to the inn included more snug bars

and upgrade to the cellars. Tracks and lanes were cobbled, extra stables built for the horses, and the yard at the back widened. By this time, The One Dog Inn had become a popular and busy coaching inn.

Further renovations made in the early and middle parts of the 19th-century, much of which remains today, included the addition of two round towers built in the Neo-Gothic style, added to the wings in 1853.

At the beginning of the 20th-century, the back yard was used by a local theatrical group known as The Curious Bottle Players, audiences watching performances from the balconies which line that side of the building. The inn was also home to a secretive order called The Lively Shadow Brotherhood (so secretive that not much is known about it); as well as being a favourite meeting place for famous artists, writers and composers of the day including the author Maurice Ringwood, the painter Lida Solvadar; and Cora Bellingham with her fiancé, the influential violinist Ernest Louis Charleston[10].

The surrounding grounds were landscaped in the 1930s under the direction of Sir Wilmott Bamble to include the addition of paved promenades and walkways, and the lake dredged followed by the construction of a boathouse.

Electrical systems were replaced or updated in the 1980s along with outside lighting; the bathrooms refurbished in the early 1990s. A horse chestnut tree, overhanging the ancient flint wall in one of the beer gardens for over 100 years, was felled, having become stricken with bleeding canker. The stables beyond the gardens were renovated in 1998 to become the Fable Stable Restaurant and facilities of the inn further enhanced by the addition of another garden seating area behind.

3 Architecture and Features [edit]
A notable feature of The One Dog Inn is the cobbles in the archway leading to the yard and stables which are made out of a dense wood. This was done to muffle the sound of horses' hooves, ensuring there would be no disturbance to any guests sleeping in their rooms upstairs.

The main building including its towers, is black and white and timber-framed with rosemary clay tiled roofs. The inn rises to two storeys with dormer windows on both sides. There are 33 rooms, each one a different design. Nine of the bedrooms have 4-poster beds. Bathrooms are fitted with modern amenities. All ceilings have thick wooden beams; windows are made of wood frames, those situated at the back being diamond-paned leaded windows. The north-facing elevation has an eight-window range to the upper storey, with attic space above, showing both vertical and curved black laths. The upper storey is jettied, the section extending over the yard entrance (former stable area), supported on wooden columns with brackets and cross-beams. There is brick facing to part of the north-face section. The chimneys are made of limestone.

Inside, there are dark oak beams and struts, and a grand stone fireplace surround in the Red Mare bar, embellished with leaf and vine decorations. The wells discovered were blocked off and secret passages found in the inn also blocked, entrances converted into sculpted wood panels. The Quiet Howl Bar features an inglenook fireplace. Other low-panelled rooms on the ground floor contain large Tudor fireplaces and cast iron dog grates. Some of the original antique chairs still used in the bars and snugs were made from ships' timbers elaborately carved with emblems and crests.

Many of the walls of the upstairs rooms were panelled in chestnut-coloured oak during the 18th-century additions. Some of these panels still show the names, dates and monograms scratched without ceremony into them by unruly guests over the centuries. Other wood incisions are better inscribed in rooms downstairs, as if they had been commissioned by artisans of the period. Notable examples are Latin phrases cut in the beams of The Look-away Bar such as *cavete numen fortis* and *ora majoris portas signatas*. Similar calligraphic chiselling was discovered on the underside of a floor plank in the main dining room by electricians during repair of wiring in 1985.

4 Haunting and other Phenomena [edit]
The One Dog Inn is well known for its hauntings over the years with much documentation available. It has been featured in articles for Vision & Shade magazine[11], and staff have been interviewed for the popular television programme Hidden Souls[12]. Derek Fileman, one of the owners of The

One Dog Inn and who has worked there since early 1993, states: "Personally I have not seen a ghost nor experienced any similar happenings, but have met a few convincing guests with their eerie tales."

It is said that a mistress of a member of The Stone Wall Gang haunts the inn by surprising the kitchen staff, when her spectre is seen walking through a bricked-up door; although this has been disputed recently by the editor of Vision & Shade magazine who claims the report is based on fiction, having been taken from a short story called The Stone Wall Lady written by the writer Valerie Webb in 1913.

In 1954, after a room maid opened a tiny window used for ventilation and looked through it to the wooden cobbles below, she saw the outline of a running dog made from the hue variations in the wood. Twenty years later, a guest reported seeing the same phenomenon though this was while riding a bicycle through the archway.

In the 1990s, an inn employee explained that while she was cleaning an upstairs bedroom, five books slid from the mantlepiece of their own accord, one after the other. And while tending to vase decorations on the fireplace hearth, she claims to have heard noises coming from behind one of the panelled walls including scratching sounds and frightening voices. This last experience caused her so much upset she resigned from her job.

The wavering ghost of a twisted old man (his skin made of

bark or tree roots) has been seen sitting in the beer garden (formally the yard) holding a horse switch in each hand.

Lights in the cellar area are switched on or off followed by the echoed sound of footsteps walking away.

A bolted door to The Candlelit Snug bar is found unbolted and left wide open the following morning, and the antique lanterns lit.

The majority of unexplained occurrences in the bedrooms have been reported as happening at night.

Room 23 (The Beaming Moon) is said to be haunted by a lady wearing old fashioned clothes, there seen in either pink or scarlet, standing by the fireplace and apparently shouting (although no voice is ever heard) with her head turned up towards the chimney flue.

Room 26 (The Colour-Me-Quick Suite) is often affected by unexpected happenings; in particular, guests reporting their clothes hung in wardrobes as being inexplicably hot despite no radiator or vent nearby.

Room 28 (Charming Horse Suite) has often been reported to be smelling of acrid spices such as nutmeg or aromatic cloves and even, on another occasion, a guest complaining of the inability to stop sneezing due to the warm and peppery fragrances in her bedroom. The present kitchen manager said that such pungent spices are rarely used in cooking although even if they were, it would be surprising for such exotic odours to travel so far, seeing as Room 28 is on the other side of the building to the kitchens.

Room 19 (Tun's Secret) is named after Thomas Tun, one of the notorious smugglers inhabiting the inn in the 18th-century. This room is said to be haunted by the ghost of a woman who is seen spinning in a captain's chair; guests have reported waking with a start in the middle of the night to find the room icy cold; others have seen the chair spinning on its own; another tells of hearing an ordinary but warning utterance, with the words spoken, "You will never know". The last guest hearing this was so distressed by the phantom voice that she "spent the whole night in the bathroom, a striped pillow wrapped tightly about my head to block my ears."

A bulky antique candle, protected under a glass jar, sits on a shelf in The Tree Bark Snug which, legend tells, burned for 300 years without melting any of its red wax.

Supernatural events explained as happening in or around the courtyard have been described as "the most baffling of apparitions and episodes".

Cellar keepers over many centuries have reported the same incident, happening at least once every five to ten years: within the brick-coved cellars directly beneath the courtyard, standing wine racks – even those heavy and high ones made of mahogany – are seen to tremble and shake, the carefully arranged bottles of wine clunking in compartments or chinking together; and larger barrels on their sides sent rolling back and forth. All severely affected by strong vibrations, as if produced from something as big as a freight train travelling overhead. This is documented to last from betweens 12 seconds up to 4 minutes.

One of the most enduring of local legends and woven into folklore concerning the inn, is known by names including Fire Dog Shadow, Swift Red, Scorching Shadow and more. Much has been written about The Shadow for centuries, the earliest mention on record from 1303, explained as "the fleeting shadowy one". There have been many other claimed sightings of The Shadow from the middle of the 16th-century onwards, described over time as a spectre, an apparition, shady substance and a visitant.

At least three people have claimed that The Shadow could communicate although with an untranslatable language. Others have mentioned that it could change shape as well as shade, appearing as a yellow and red flame flickering across the courtyard paving accompanied by a ticking noise, the sound described by one person in the 19th-century "as if made by claws of metal".

Because the courtyard is open to the sky, it's perhaps surprising to hear that no bird of any variety has ever been seen within its confines. That is, apart from a reported occurrence in the summer of 1948: the courtyard filled with chattering birds of many types – ravens, starlings, finches, gulls, etc. Each bird had stood or perched on a bottle end for an hour, before all rising up and out of the courtyard with tremendous flapping of wings, described as sounding like claps of thunder.

*****

Stella, if I tell you I saw what is described as The Fire Dog Shadow, you definitely will think I'm making it up, on top of what else I'm going to say. But I did see it—and I'm not making it up, I swear. Under the circumstances, adding a paranormal element to other radical incidents is almost expected in a way. Whatever this is about, it's become like unknown forces over a long period of time were "given an inch, but took a mile". Oh, I know what I mean.

There's a corridor running the length of one side of the courtyard with panelled picture windows looking into it. So when I chased one of those dogs along the corridor, I saw – despite only seeing its form from the periphery of my vision – what can only be described as a ghost of a shadow. It was like red smoke, billowing and convulsing, at times in the shape of a large dog. It moved fast over the inner walls of the courtyard, above the other real dog which was barking and growling constantly. Sometimes it was clear that this ghost-smoke shadow-creature was running, but with its legs moving in slow motion despite its apparent speed along those walls. And this apparition, or whatever it was, would vanish if I looked directly at it through a window. Now isn't that just one of the strangest things you've ever heard?

Getting rather late now so I'll tell more tomorrow (then I'll backtrack a bit – that previous paragraph was jumping the gun). No need to reply to this if you don't want to; maybe you'll have questions after tomorrow's email though, we wait to see. Goodnight, from Audrey

•

Email From: Audrey Ackerman 04 June 2013 19:48
To: Stella Bridgeport Re: Two dogs at The One Dog Inn

Evening, Stella, I trust everything went well at the Centre today. I was sitting at home this afternoon and wanted to come in – so I must be feeling better – but best to keep it the way we agreed, for at least another week, I know.

Let us continue. Once more will I warn you that what you are about to read will be inconceivable but you have to believe it, for my sake. Please, please try, Stella, it will help me enormously. We were talking about the events of last Wednesday: I'm driving along the white road which leads up to the inn, grassed areas with their groups of trees, old-fashioned lamp standards and paths either side; the inn up ahead, and the lake partly hidden, to its right.

The One Dog Inn kept on catching my eye. I felt compelled to look, appearing as if it was lit with a yellow sunlight despite the morning's sun hidden by cloud cover. With the inn's long black and white frontage and red tiled roofs in the middle distance looking just like a very large doll's house, I became drawn to it. I pressed on the accelerator, now driving well over the 15 mph speed limit. And the sudden appeal was accompanied by a sense of elation. This was because no matter how much closer I became, the inn remained the same size. It was as if I could wind down the car's window and extend an arm to take hold of one side of it; swing open the frontage to expose its miniature rooms, all perfectly furnished with tiny furniture.

This certain fascination was not enough to hold me. Toy boats on the lake took my attention then — at least, I thought they might be toy boats.

Trying to explain this further: as I drove closer to The One Dog Inn, it, and the objects floating on the lake, didn't change their size (although everything else did, as is normal). And this continued for a minute or so until, without warning, when I was no more than twenty yards away, these things – that is, the inn, and the lake with its toy boats – suddenly became their actual size. But now, travelling those last few yards onward, I realized the toy boats were nothing of the sort. They were swans on that lake, and they grew to enormous size very quickly. Did I hear any popping or suction noise? Don't think I did but might as well have done – seeming appropriate at that moment of quick change. Can reality pop?

Whatever, by the time I drove towards the gravelled area at the front of the inn, those waterbirds were massive, about six or seven of them, each one at least twenty-five feet high. Like plastic gondolas of exquisite and surprising detail, every feather delicately rendered, each swan moving at a gentle rate across the rippling lake. Then I could almost believe I had a brain fugue via an infected ear when one of them, then another straight after, lifted and outstretched their massive wings, beautiful curved necks bent backwards, the ochre yellow beaks opening and closing. I was so enthralled that I stopped the car. Now I must underline the fact that although this was as if from a breathtaking technicolor dream, it was rooted in reality; everything else about, as normal as the day. Remember I'm considering the grounds of The One Dog Inn as being the set for a film? The swans must have been expensive, complex, cleverly crafted, animatronic machines.

I tore my sight from them, started the car and carried on, past the front of the inn, over to its left where there's a car park. I parked up and walked over the gravel towards one of the inn's side entrances. That was when my attention was caught again, this time by a line of trees acting as a divider between two of the parking areas. Although not as spectacular as the huge swans, still those trees were another surreal display. They were ancient specimens, perhaps 200 years old or more, all with large moss-speckled trunks and their heavy branches laden with apples. And I mean laden – clusters of five or six everywhere, along every branch length. Each apple appeared to be a ripened fruit ready for picking despite the month being May; each one identical (as far as I could make out). Not only in size but also colouring – half red gradating to green. More than likely no wasp scars or insect holes, just perfectly formed, every one. Convincing to look at; it must have taken a long time to decorate the trees with the apples. So what with this and the gigantic swans, science fiction filmset is seeming a good answer, you agree?

I'm going to leave it there and carry on tomorrow. I might even attach a few of that writer's files as well, for interest. Though a last thing to mention: as I approached the old blackened door of the ivy-streaked inn, I heard heavy footsteps on the gravel. It was a jogger, running towards me. Bye for now, hope you have a pleasant evening. Audrey

•

Email From: Stella Bridgeport 04 June 2013 21:13
To: Audrey Ackerman Re: Two dogs at The One Dog Inn

Evening, Audrey. I'll make it quick if that's OK. Need to prepare a few things this evening for the Centre tomorrow.

I've known you for six years. I like you, in fact can say I love you as a friend. We've had our ups and downs. But in the main, always got on swimmingly, haven't we. Not been many secrets. And in all that time, you've been consistent. With a high quality of work, professional attitude, caring manner. Always being even-tempered and patient. Never given any indication you'd backbite or cause problems just for the sake of it. Did I need say so much? Probably not. But the reason I did is to underline my utter confusion with what's going on. Can't believe you're having a joke. Or trying to confuse me on purpose. Still, what you've written seems utterly out-of-the-ordinary (in a big way). Knocked me off balance in a sense.

Blow the reports. They can be done on Thursday now. (Put them off so many times, a couple more days won't matter).

You asked I didn't make judgements or give explanations. Yet in your last email you're asking what I think again. Going to run with that. Possibly offend you once more but I believe (in fact I know) our strength of friendship can weather it.

So quite a story so far, what with hauntings and other supernatural goings-on. (Only read that section from the CycloWik entry you sent. Sorry, didn't have time to read the other parts). Shadow dogs seen running round the courtyard. One Dog Inn looking like a doll's house. Huge popping swans on the lake. And thousands of apples on the apple trees, all alike. Interesting stuff in its own way, I suppose, even if a bit spooky.

A thought came to mind. Going to be bold enough to tell you what it is. Could be wrong, could be right. Please just take time to consider before jumping down my throat. Will you do that? But first to say, I'm not buying this filmset explanation. A few reasons, none of which I'll labour you with. Back to my theory: involves you're new friend, Dennis. You said how distant he's been recently. Absent-minded, a dreamer? And he's a chemist, isn't he. I'm just surmising that a chemist has access to all sorts of drugs.

I'm about 15 years older than you, Audrey. Old enough to remember the '70s scenes. Wasn't involved in any big way. Went to a few discos, saw bands playing, the usual. Always managed to steer myself away from situations involving illegal drugs. Still learnt about them, enough to be wary, you know, the psychedelic ones, etc. You were out with Dennis on

Monday night, you told me? Not saying he spiked your drink or anything. But surely the possibility something got there by accident? Something from the chemist that by chance fell into his jacket and fell out again? Do you remember what you were drinking? Did it taste funny, can you remember?

If not that, could be a drug of one sort or other got into your food on Tuesday. Or even in your breakfast Wednesday morning.

Get it? Giant swans, identical apples, running ghost dogs, visual quirks. Indications you were hallucinating under the influence of a hallucinogenic drug. And as much as I've learned, once the drug is diluted in your bloodstream, there's no permanent damage to mind or body. What do you say?
Best regards, Stella

•

Email From: Audrey Ackerman 04 June 2013 22:23
To: Stella Bridgeport Re: Two dogs at The One Dog Inn

HOW DARE YOU! CRYINH SO MUCH CAN BARELYVTYPE YOU ARE ATROCIOUS STELLA NEVER CONSIFERED YOU TO BE SO HORRIBLE JUSTLEAVE ME ALONE

•

Email From: Stella Bridgeport 04 June 2013 22:47
To: Audrey Ackerman Please contact me

Had to phone. Late for phoning, I do know. Robert told me

off but had to. Hung on for ages waiting for you to lift the receiver, so apologies if ringing got on your nerves. Can understand why you're not picking up the phone. But I wish you would. I'll try again tomorrow. Come on Audrey, we need to talk this through. Kind regards, Stella

•

Email From: Stella Bridgeport 05 June 2013 18:55
To: Audrey Ackerman Phone call

Hello Audrey, picking up the receiver and putting it back down again, then leaving it off the hook isn't helping either of us. Just want to speak to you. I've reread my email where I mention Dennis. Think you misunderstood the part when I wrote about drugs in your food and drink. I was throwing out the possibility of an accident. That's all, a wild guess. Otherwise if no influence from a drug, then what? The filmset idea? Might sound harsh but I don't buy that, as I said. Would be in the local papers. And what film would involve identical apples and massive plastic birds?

Here is honesty. When I read your descriptions it seemed like you were piling one thing on top of another. Building a giddy tower of fantastical nonsense. I had to tell you, that's how it came across.

I have an extra idea. Food poisoning adversely affecting your sight, what with the tiny then big building, etc. But forget that too, I know you won't entertain it. Another one: those apple trees, a prolific variety that produces a couple of months earlier than usual. Maybe created with genetic engineering. You know what scientists are like nowadays. I'm surprised wheat doesn't come in red and white stripes and smell of juniper. Seem to be doing whatever they want nowadays, all this modifying, don't they.

Let's talk about those swans. You agree there's more than one possible explanation, yes? So I'll throw this into the ring. They were made as a tourist attraction to get more customers. But I'll admit something now. I left work earlier than I should this afternoon. I talked Robert into driving me to your house. We parked outside. I changed my mind about knocking on your door.

Then we drove to Legatemead. Not trying to test you, just wanted to see these giant swans for myself. Don't know if you know, you can see across Gone-But-Not-Forgotten to the inn's lake from a gap in bushes along Camberside Road. Have to tell you, Audrey, there weren't any swans that we could see, large or small, even with binoculars. Perhaps they're pulled on ropes. Lined up behind the boathouse for the evening. Still trying to get this. Want you happy with an explanation so we're back on track.

Where from here? You continue to ignore me? We go our separate ways when it comes to friendship? Please don't, Audrey, I'll miss you. We've had lovely times, haven't we, in the Centre and out. A great shame to throw that away all because of a few misunderstandings. Hope you agree.

Please carry on, talk to me via emails again. Send that author's file if you like. Tell me more about the jogger perhaps. But mainly tell me you're OK. Best regards, Stella

•

Email From: Audrey Ackerman 06 June 2013 14:39
To: Stella Bridgeport Re: Phone call

Stella, for the record, I never said Dennis was distant with me. I don't know where you got that from either, you seem to be making things up. I mentioned he was a quiet man who does find it difficult to start a conversation. He's shy, that's all. And even then, he's opening up compared to our first date a couple of months back (when he took me to that overpriced restaurant in Barnford. Remember I told you I had the last of a cold and my teeth were aching? So now you get it why there wasn't much chatting?). Over the past few weeks, we talk more; and getting on well together, touch wood. And I have to correct you: he's not a chemist, he's a pharmacist. There's a difference.

I'll admit, I misunderstood your email about psychedelic drugs. I read your words as nasty, implying horrid things about Dennis. I thought you accused him of drugging me; and was insulting to a high degree, playing my emotions like a yo-yo. On top of that, I was beginning to believe you were in league with someone else, both determined to drive me insane. You can understand why I went ballistic. I've been clutching at straws for answers to my out-of-this-world experiences; you've been consistent in blaming faults with my brain cells.

Though finally you supplied a logical answer – concerning apples and genetics – this does click, makes sense. If they were really there, not imagined, then it could well have been a wild experiment, true. (Especially as those apples were growing from the branches of oak trees). Same with that dog's eyes – a genetic experiment gone horribly wrong or even a successful one created by morally vacant scientists. Then again, maybe these things weren't there at all. What if I am developing some terrible neurological disorder that's begun affecting perceptions in a major way – seeing giant swans that aren't there and the rest? And if that's really happening, why is the world seeming to have gone back to normal? Or do I now think what's normal is nothing of the kind? Is that the subtle sliding into madness? The heavily-built jogger running towards me, his black and blue tracksuit stained with sweat, and spattered with streaks of blood and mud. The ungainly way he moved forward with one of his ankles the size of a small balloon, the foot at an obscure angle. His weight was falling onto the edge of that foot bulging from his trainer, leg flesh showing as purple. And each time this happened, a jolt of pain seen flashing across his already screwed up face contorted with agony and exhaustion, a type of revulsion as if he'd witnessed a dread horror. When stepping out of his way as he made a beeline for me, thick words juddering from his twisted mouth as a hoarse phrase: "Can't stop". Then the howling as he jogged on in his lopsided, hunched and jumpy way, towards the left hand side of The One Dog Inn before disappearing around the corner towards the trees with apples: perhaps all that was a nightmarish creation made from inside my head. And yet in one of the files from the memory stick

I've been reading, it mentions a jogger who was running the same gravel path, wearing the same style of tracksuit.

You mentioned honesty. Here's some: I feel so miserable and anxious right now. I wish I'd never gone to that One Dog Inn. I wish I could sleep properly again.

•

Email From: Stella Bridgeport 06 June 2013 18:48
To: Audrey Ackerman Re: Phone call

Audrey, listen to me and listen well. You've got to get a grip of yourself. Otherwise you WILL land up in a psychiatric ward. That's telling it straight, for your own good. I'm not in league with anyone. And not trying to harm you. Your experiences are beyond understanding but you must not let it rip you apart like this. Start sending the man's files then. I'll study them, promise.

And the jogger: when I read more about him, there'll be no judgements, no opinions. That's all I'll say right now on that score.

This is what I recommend. Hot milk, tuck yourself up in bed. Listen to a soothing radio station. Read a gentle book even. Try to empty your mind of it all. And when you do lay down to sleep, just think of nice things. You know, like a past holiday. Laying under a beach umbrella. An unspoiled sky, clean sand and gentle sea waves. That kind of thing. Bye for now, Stella

•

Email From: Audrey Ackerman 07 June 2013 15:12
To: Stella Bridgeport Files 4 attachments

Hello Stella, I took your advice to the letter. (Well, almost – I read magazines and a few more files from the memory stick rather than a book; discovered a rather lovely radio station that plays relaxing, ambient-type music through the night. Called Tranquil FM if you'd like to check it out).

Don't worry about me any more, I'll be alright. I mustn't get so uptight about everything otherwise it will affect me badly, you're correct again. I've been overwrought, I really have to calm myself. Though it's been so frustrating not knowing what it's all about.

I'll still get the other events out of my system and tell you what else happened on that morning. I'll restrain myself from reading any more from the memory stick for a while. You did say you don't mind reading them though: here's some of Gideon Hadley's files, starting from the second batch. (In the first batch, the author mixes story ideas with the day's happenings, in diary and journal form; including personal thoughts and much mention of his wife Nicole. Those first files are dated from a few weeks before he and Nicole are guests at The One Dog Inn). Hope you find interest in the second lot I've attached. Please let me know if or when you want to read more. Best regards, Audrey

P.S Just thought, I'll summarize those first files here, to bring things into perspective for when you read the ones I'm sending. Right, it seems that the earliest date of any of the files on the memory stick is Saturday 4th May this year. That's about a month ago, isn't it. Gideon Hadley talks about pressure he's feeling to accomplish the writing of another novel in such a "ridiculously" short space of time; how his literary agent always pushes him too much; how he's beginning to feel much stress. On top of this, it seems there are quite a few problems between him and his wife Nicole. She appears to be complaining often about his unsociable work hours typing his words, how he's always in the library and museums, or visiting a university campus (places for his inspiration & research). And unhappy about lack of understanding concerning their daughter Amelie who, apparently, lives in a student flat in a dangerous part of a city (in Russex, I gathered).

It gets to a peak a few days later. Nicole – described as becoming "distant, aloof and even spiteful on occasions" – has threatened to move out of their apartment (seems not for the first time). Gideon is torn between trying to stop his wife from leaving, and finding time for research and notes needed for his fifth science fiction novel, enough to satisfy his publisher that progress is being made. At this point he does seem to have priorities wrong. Then follows a couple of days where he describes how not much is done or resolved. This is followed by a description of how he (Gideon) almost pleads with Nicole to give him a second chance, after she decides to stay with a friend (a female friend or so she tells him). He's furious but despondent. That's the first files in a nutshell.

This strained and volatile relationship seems doomed to me, especially when I read details concerning his wife's previous "indiscretions" with a particular man (though Gideon has never been able to find out this other person's name, or even if he exists). He explains to himself the possibility that Nicole is trying to make him jealous by creating a fictitious person. Along with this, every time Nicole leaves the house, even going to the shops, Gideon becomes suspicious again. And all the while, he needs to prepare for the new novel. (I know that's more work than it sounds, even for my humble books it was harder than I thought). Don't have to read much to see it begins to tear his mind up. There's a lot to insinuate he's being pushed to depression. Then suddenly a diary note explaining his intentions to ask Nicole to go away with him for a few weeks, to the peace and quiet of the countryside; for them to work together to resolve differences and to rekindle their romance. All very bitter sweet in its own way.

Copious ideas for his new novel too. He's decided on its title: NanoSynthetica. I couldn't read a book called that, could you? Suppose there must be readers out there who would though. Also complicated scientific notes concerning quantum stuff, and nanotechnology involving "organic and synthetic artificially intelligent components". All above my head, I'm afraid. I Googled nanotech: something to do with building machines at atomic levels. Still none the wiser.

Last thing to mention before I go: I can't work out why that grey dog dug up a cigar tin (with the memory stick inside) within the courtyard. Was it just a coincidence? But then dogs aren't stupid, are they. There's always a reason for an animal to dig, and it does seem like the memory stick was what he wanted me to have. But why? And where now is the owner of it, the writer of the files, Gideon Hadley? Still a guest at The One Dog Inn? Why would he have buried a memory stick with his journal entries in the first place? And a related thought: I did wonder if those two dogs were owned by Gideon and Nicole, although there's no mention of pets in any of the file pages. So many questions which I guess will never be answered. Even Miss Maypole couldn't work it all out. Bye again, kind regards, Audrey

•

Email From: Stella Bridgeport 07 June 2013 19:47
To: Audrey Ackerman Re: Files on the memory stick

Thanks for files. I'll read them after my drama. (Third and final part of Bringing the Storm at 9pm. Gripping, terrific performances from Celia Thorpe. Can highly recommend. Bound to be repeated so keep an eye out for it).

Really glad you're feeling stronger, Audrey. Nothing like a restful night for recuperation. Idea: have a break away for a couple of days. B&B in Stokesflown perhaps, get some sea air. Eat fish and chips along the promenade. Play fruit machines on the pier! Just a thought. I know how much you like the seaside. Kind Regards, Stella

*****

Attachment 1 : JourneyToGo ReadMe.txt
3 files exported in session : Sat 18 May to Sun 19 May 2013
Gideon's Journal & latest notes for novel (NanoS)

Attachment 2 : Journal+NanoS notes 20/5.pdf
Monday 20 May 2013 14:09
Journal: Been faffing around for too long, must get in gear soon. Haven't contacted Phyllis yet, or Gregory Samsan for that matter, to let them know my plan of action over the next couple of weeks. And still no packing done. Nicole is more organized than I am; always packs her suitcase at least 2 or 3 days before it's needed. I'll leave mine till the last minute, every time – hard to break old habits.

Looking back to last week, I was shocked at Nicole's opinion after telling her we needed a trip somewhere to recharge our batteries, get things into perspective. Maybe shocked is too strong a word; I certainly was surprised. Too keen? Not sure what I mean by that except to say I was expecting resistance to the idea and having to convince her to come away with me. But she seemed happy; even saying this morning how much she's looking forward to the break. Avoided any conversation about "relationship cracks" though.

Although Nicole made it clear that she doesn't want me working on my novel while we're away, she did concede that writing the journal is important for me as a catalyst for creating ideas. At least she's relented on that score; and cancelled the stay with her friend. Postponed the beach house visit too. (She couldn't have stayed there anyway, I'm renting it – must have slipped her mind. The Evagales heaves with tourists in May; she knows that).

I'll type a few more NanoS notes then email Phyllis and GS. Actually, might be better to phone Gregory. And phone the inn, find out when the room's ready tomorrow. (Plus check they've put the champagne and flowers there).

NS Notes: Quintessence Industries is finding their face cream so popular, they need even more factories to match demand. SkinSyn, made with patented nanotechnology, is becoming the biggest selling product in the world.

Then sales skyrocket when a system is invented which not only alters skin cells for a perfect complexion, but also users are able to communicate with the nanobots under the skin to produce starling results. With electrodes and an encephalographic device as interface, the SkinSyn nanobots can be fine-tuned using a program called SynMorph. Eventually the system becomes even more sophisticated: users are able to alter many parameters; not only to adjust skin pigment but change texture too, even perfume. The more radical users choose to have their face skin as patterned leather, powdered metals or even multi-layered tree bark. To revert to their own natural colour and texture, they reprogram using personal default settings, the changes accomplished in a matter of days.

Chapter 9 will now start with Jimp Pallinberg hacking SynMorph to open up even more exciting possibilities for user programming of the nanobots.

Remember: Petra from Daley's is picking up the Jaggerson early evening. There's only the slimmest of chances it'll be mended before midday, so I'm resigned to the fact we'll be travelling to the inn tomorrow in Nicole's car.

Attachment 3 : Journal+NanoS notes 21/5.pdf
Tuesday 21 May 2013 12:18
Journal: A few quick jottings on the laptop before lunch. Been here an hour; now sat in the so-called Candlelit Snug bar with a nice pint of Oysterman's Thunderclap. I've had their Rumbledown before but not this one – hints of ginger and honey with just the subtlest bitter twang at the end. Very nice. The bar is cosy without any windows, black-painted infills between the even blacker beams, with lit candles on the barrels. Mock sawdust on the floor. Picturesque. Nicole finished her glass of wine ten minutes ago and decided to wander around. It is a very interesting old building, after all.

Nicole opted to drive this morning; in fact, she insisted. She seemed in a particularly buoyant mood. I hope we go from strength to strength from now; clear the baggage and clutter, start fresh, move forward together with a renewed, invigorated relationship.

Uneventful journey down, other than a hold-up for twenty minutes along the M769, just outside of Halleyton. Before we hit Paxbury, I spotted a couple of kestrels flying horizontally in a spiral, one following the other across the cloudless sky. Never seen that sort of behaviour before.

Legatemead is more like an overgrown village (perhaps a definition of a town anyway). A pleasant green, and quaint-looking shops on all four sides of Farmer's Market Square. When I read earlier about the puzzling epitaph to be found just off of the market area, I knew we'd have to stop for a look. On a lone tombstone found along Coptical Street – in a tended square of grass hemmed by quartz boulders – can be found chiselled into its weathered face: "Ne'er to reverse thy creator". Took a snap of it and talked Nicole out of the car to have a cuppa in the Spotadog Tearooms next door. Inside the tearoom she quickly reverted to her snapping self but seemed to cheer up again when we set off to drive the last half mile to The One Dog Inn.

Thought I caught sight of Nicole poking her head around the corner into the bar – maybe I didn't. In three quarters of an hour or so we'll grab a bite to eat, by which time our room should be ready.

Impressive wrought iron gates to the inn's grounds. Too late to take a picture – swung open quicker than I thought. A lovely setting; slow drive up to the inn, plenty to see either side: landscaped lawns, terraces and garden areas with elaborate lampposts, large stone flower urns and an abundance of benches.

Looked a fine lake too, swans floating on its unruffled surface over by a green-painted boathouse. Worth a stroll beside it this evening, I considered.

Parked the car; decided to leave the luggage in the boot till we've access to the room. A line of massive oak trees leads up to a pergola-covered path which took us to one of the front entrances.

When we walked over to the reception desk, the woman behind it made eye-contact with Nicole and smiled as if with recognition. A good receptionist always makes guests feel welcome, I know, and I wouldn't have thought more of it until she said, "Hello, Mrs. Hadley, nice to see you." Then I would have sworn that Nicole gave the quickest of head shakes. With her generous smile dropped, the receptionist looked me up and down in a condescending manner. I was inclined to say, "What's your problem?" but kept quiet; although I did ask Nicole, 'Have you been here before?' She didn't seem to hear.

The receptionist informed us that our room would be ready at 2pm, her broad smile returning as if deciding she'd mistaken me for a previously unpleasant customer. Whatever, I could have considered this was for Nicole's benefit, as if to "keep the peace".

I was never the suspicious sort until Nicole had her affair – or didn't have an affair, who damn well knows. Whether she did or didn't, I've been developing a habit of reading into situations too deeply, I do know.

The room not ready for a couple of hours was the perfect excuse for us to have a midday drink. Which I'll carry on with now: another swift gulp of my ale.

NS Notes: SynMorph becomes largest software download ever on the planet. Users swapping their personal settings, and tampering of the software and electronic interfaces, triggers a devastating effect worldwide: SkinSyn nanobots begin to develop a type of hive consciousness.

Dreadful accidents are occurring: users are reporting that replacement skin tissue by the nanobots has become synthetic and irreplaceable: it's now impossible to go back to the original organic cellular structures, the skin and underlying muscles now silicon-based. Those affected become known as afflicted with SkinSyn Syndrome.

Enter Beck Sammett, a world-leading nanotechnology scientist, contacted by Ellie McPearson who suffers from

SkinSyn Syndrome. She has discovered a way to reverse the process by rewriting the SkinMorph code, though she believes it would need a central mainframe computer to initiate the process. She asks Beck Sammett to convince Quintessence Industries that this is what must be done. He readily agrees.

Nicole is back from her walk. Time for lunch, I'm thinking; or another pint, whichever comes first.

Attachment 4 : Journal+NanoS notes 21/5.pdf
Tuesday 21 May 2013 11:29
Journal: Very good room; most pleased with it. The only reservation I have is the two leaded windows are high up so although they let through adequate light, they can't be looked through. Attractive engravings and prints on the walls. Nicole seemed to appreciate the bunch of flowers and bottle of champagne. InterFlower certainly went to town for me.

Nicole and I even had a cuddle tonight before she went to sleep in this delightful four-poster. There are heavy drapes from its top rungs; posts beautifully turned and carved with daisies. A plush carpet; the bedroom is at least five times larger than ours at home. High and imposing marble fireplace inset with porcelain tiles; half wood panelling on the walls – in mahogany, I think – the top half wallpapered with flower patterns; heavy beams running across the whitewashed ceiling. A couple of nice antique chairs, a writing desk, old-fashioned brass floor lamp; TV, tea and coffee making facilities, the usual there. Nice size bathroom too with a roll top bath. Excellent for the price.

We decided to have lunch in the beer garden. The sun was

almost scorching so early in the afternoon but we persevered, sitting at a table under an umbrella.

The potted mackerel was enjoyable, so was the bacon & avocado poppy-seeded roll. Nicole ordered a side salad – that's all she wanted. Another glass of ale for me. Well, it would have been rude not to…

Got the keys to Room 19 from the receptionist who was still offish with me. Perhaps she doesn't like men with long hair tied in a ponytail. Could be the beard; who knows.

Fetched the luggage and found a member of staff — she found another staff member to help me with the suitcases up the stairs to the bedroom.

On the way back to the beer garden, just before turning into the archway, a jogger almost bowled me over: a guy in a blue and black tracksuit hurtling along the gravel path. "Can't stop," he shouted out while giving a particularly annoying grin. I'll give him can't stop.

The stroll along the promenade path in the evening was delightful: low sun streaking the lake with orange, bollard lights hyphenating the lake's edge like a yellow necklace, broken by magnolia trees and weeping willow. Near the boathouse, rowing boats moored between two jetties, side by side as neatly as sardines in a tin. A huddle of swans congregated by bullrushes as we made our way back to an algae-slimed retaining wall. Ducks sat with eyes closed, warming their breasts and webbed feet on the fading day's heated grass. Then gentle sounds from plucked strings of a mandolin from a folk group playing in one of the bars. We went back inside; and there we spent a pleasant rest of the evening listening to The Blue Pheasants.

Might go back into Legatemead main town tomorrow or further afield for the afternoon, we'll see.

NS Notes: The SkinSyn nanobots are now able to replicate and replace organs of the body by transforming each cell into a silicon equivalent.

People are fighting back the best they can by unhooking from the program. But it's too late: any changes in their bodies can no longer be rectified; and with the nanobots acquired hive intelligence, they have their own complex program – to replace every single cell in the entire body with silicon and metallic equivalents. Even the blood of users will eventually be replaced with an oil-like liquid.

Ellie McPearson convinces Beck Sammett that he will be the saviour of the world by initiating the cure for SkinSyn Syndrome by running the supercomputer program within Quintessence Industries.

*****

Email From: Audrey Ackerman 08 June 2013 16:32
To: Stella Bridgeport Re: Files on the memory stick

Good advice again, Stella, the B&B. I will consider that, I do like to be beside the seaside :) Although I'm itching to get back to the Centre soon – I am missing it all, you know. I'll see how I feel, beginning of next week.

Dennis seemed upset yesterday; all I could say was I won't be seeing him for a few days or more but couldn't bring myself to give reasons. Just said I'll miss him and needed time on my own to think. Of course, he assumed that involved us. It must have taken twenty minutes to explain that it didn't have anything to do with our relationship. I'm almost certain he finally believed me – I hope so.

I wonder what you made of those files, Stella. See what I mean about that jogger? And he mentions the receptionist. Though no explanation of what I encountered when I met her, other than a shivery similarity with his descriptions for that science fiction novel. You still don't know what I'm saying there, mentioning the receptionist that way. I'll try an explanation as clearly as I can. It's still so vivid in my mind: the following description is another crazy, surreal occurrence which happened on that Wednesday morning.

I'll interrupt myself at this point to address the possibility that you've insinuated I've been winding you up over a course of emails, for whatever reason. You know I write essays and factual stories about animals. Not much of an imagination for fiction. So to say, if I really wanted to confuse you using imaginative stories, I wouldn't be very successful. A couple of ideas now, try these: fireworks from the chimneys. Giant giraffes eating leaves growing out of the inn's tower windows. You see what I'm saying, a bit rubbish, aren't they.

And yet someone else's imagination has affected my reality somehow. But how does fiction impose itself upon reality? I mean to say, how is it at all possible to make pure fiction a fact, especially fantastic fiction that came from the mind of Gideon Hadley?

I can answer my question and it will be the same as yours: it's not possible – it's impossible. Despite that, when I entered the inn and went to the reception, there before my astonished eyes, seated behind the reception counter, was an animated shop window mannequin; a cleverly created android. I can't describe her – it – in any other way. Her blonde hair seemed as if made from spun nylon, strands tinted with orange and yellows, thicker hanks segmented. One side of her head was shaved. Her pupils and irises were reversed, I kid you not. It was difficult not to stare at their beauty, each iris being a jet black circle with the pupil in its middle slowly changing colour from blue to orange, to mauve and so on. The green skin of her face, pulled taut across her angular cheekbones, had an unaccountable lustre, quite unnatural; a glistening, glittering effect as if made from animated fish scales. Slender hands clasped before her, as if she wore skin-tight gloves made from metallic fibres, the digits articulated with hinged metal joints. And there was an embossed pattern of hexagons etched from the side of her symmetrical head, down to her cheek, and finishing on her neck.

Her lipstick was striped. And in neon colours which changed regularly in a pulsing fashion. Her mouth was oscillating between a pleasant smile to the forlorn downturned lips of a dejected clown while she spoke, and when she did speak, her neon lipstick sparked with diamond-shaped lights from her perfect cyan teeth. I'm not embarrassed to write any of this, Stella. I saw what I saw and heard what I heard. I'm not making it up, any of it, I swear.

Remember the robot-type voice I told you about? You've guessed: it was her voice, and it was a baffling experience hearing it again. Like a combination of those synthesizers with multiple voice frequencies. Now and then the volume altered as if she was a radio broadcaster and I was the radio listener losing and gaining reception. I remember the haunting words she spoke, similar to those spoken over the phone. After fixing me with the incredible eyes, the hexagons on her cheeks glowing and pulsating, she said repeatedly, "Are you real, am I real. Help me, help you." I could have screamed at this point with the sheer outrageous, disturbing trauma of it all. I even thought of slapping this thing pretending to be human, pretending to be a woman, to stop it from talking, stop it from frightening me with its irritating but complex tone, stop it from rasping the same phrases over and over again. Then, without thought, I did slap it across that perfect but abnormal face, and it felt like I had slapped engraved metal. She immediately stopped talking, and I heard dogs barking from somewhere further inside the inn. I backed away from that strange robot and ran through a couple of bars, then along a short corridor, my ears now attuned to those barks. As disturbing as it all was, I was there to do a job, and a sense of mission kept me going.

When passing through the bars, there were a few people sat on seats, all with drinks before them – three couples and two men I recall; and though seeming normal, it struck me that they were asleep with vacant expressions on their slack faces, their eyes glassy and distant, all still. The young barman stood behind the bar cleaning a glass with a towel with those same lost eyes, his mouth slightly open.

I know you won't be reading this email until you're home, Stella, so if you do reply later on, please don't expect an email back tonight; another early night for me. I do feel drained today but mustn't nap this afternoon otherwise it'll spoil it for later. My sleeping pattern has already been disturbed enough. I might as well plough on to the end here but with my weariness I'll try to be as brief as I can. (Still a fair amount to type but at least it'll keep me from dropping off prematurely).

So, I find the corridor which overlooks one side of the courtyard. As I look through a window, I see there's lots of overgrown bushes, weeds and dusty tables and chairs out there, like it hasn't been used for a while. All those bottles (mentioned in the Cyclowik entry) embedded in different types of stone or rock, quite fascinating in their own way. Parts of the courtyard walls have lost their cladding of whitewashed plaster and wooden battens so you can see the original courtyard was built out of flint, with added quartz and marble. I could make out subtle patterns and exotic designs there.

And in one corner were the two dogs. Large terrier types, cross-breeds I thought, one dark grey with a white ruff, the other brown. That brown one was tied to a metal hook by a length of rope. The grey dog appeared to be male; the leashed animal, female. (Obvious, isn't it, just by looking at their muzzles). They were facing each other with heads down, snarling and snapping, sounding hoarse as if they had been barking for so long they'd given themselves sore throats. I can well believe it. I should have returned to the Centre at that point, or at least phoned, to let you know my assessment of the situation but under the circumstances I wasn't thinking straight.

With my mental state so befuddled, what I did next I didn't give a second thought. These two terrier types were not much smaller than a border collie or retriever; short haired, both on the slim side. I judged them as frightened but not frightening nor particularly dangerous. Why I came to that conclusion quickly, I don't know, but trusted my sixth sense (as I always do in such situations). I found an unlocked door which opens onto the courtyard, walked out, the door closing behind me; and straight away both dogs stopped their barking.

The brown dog cowered in a corner while the grey one shot across to a clear area of paving slabs with bottle bases showing. Between the slabs were a couple of areas of earth with scruffy weeds. That's where the dog started digging frantically, head down, scraping up the soil with his two front paws. I went closer until I saw a yellow metallic object showing. Still with his head and ears low, the dog slunk away as I bent down to pick the object up. I brushed off some dirt and recognized it as a cigar tin. I opened it and inside found the memory stick. I put the tin on a bench and the memory stick in my pocket. By this time the grey dog also cowered, behind a couple of old bench umbrellas propped against a wall. It was then I had a disturbing sensation of being watched, and I don't mean by either of those two dogs; more like being scrutinized by a hidden animal while it tracks its prey.

I decided I'd seen enough and still feeling queasy, went back to the oak door and started to pull it open. I didn't spot the grey dog leap out from behind the umbrellas, and run very fast as it must have done to reach me so quickly. I stepped back, caught by surprise. That male dog was scratching at the door and before I knew it I'd pulled the door fully open. (Told you I wasn't thinking straight). It brushed past my legs. I chased the dog and saw it beside a cabinet at the end of the corridor, in shadow, with his head still down and turned towards me, this time as if waiting for me to follow. And I did follow that dog, and did see The Shadow flashing about through the windows at the corners of my eyes – the ghost dog or whatever it is, defying gravity as it ran across a wall.

After I turned my sight back to the corridor, the dog had vanished, I guessed through the open door at the end. I went through into the hall of a stairway; and looking up, heard the dog growling. While climbing those stairs, I was unafraid although concerned. And when at the top, the dog pushed past me again. I followed until it stopped, shortly after, by the open door of one of the bedrooms, padding from one side to the other, as if telling me that's where I should go. And when I reached that bedroom door I felt violently sick. If you had turned the world upside down and shook it, that wouldn't have felt half as bad as my churning stomach was making me feel, along with a thumping heart and dry dust for saliva. Then weighing heavily on top of that: as I stared at that animal, the sight took me almost to the point of tears, made me shout out in pure shock. Its eyes, the dog's awful eyes. I could sob thinking back. Got to go, sorry.

•

Email From: Audrey Ackerman 08 June 2013 17:45
To: Stella Bridgeport Re: Files on the memory stick

Apologies, Stella, got myself upset again. I've had a cup of tea and feel better. I'll finish this episode: I was compelled to enter that bedroom; a four-poster bed over to the right, a white laptop with its lid open on the duvet, and a substantial marble fireplace set into one of the walls. Another door (presumably to the bathroom) was closed; all in all, a large room but no sign of the dog. I couldn't work out where it might be hiding.

Then I ran out of the room, back to the staircase landing, almost falling to the bottom of the stairs, found an exit and ran back to the car, yanked the door open then sat crying and crying. Eventually I calmed down just enough to phone you; that's when you couldn't grasp what I was saying. But I do see now – how could you begin to get the drift from my tearful babble? You made me so angry at the time though it helped dry the tears, enough for me to drive home. That's when I sent you my first email about wanting to resign.

The whole lot is cuckoo, I realize, but please don't say I had food poisoning, went mad or was drugged up any more, Stella, I won't be able to handle it. There's nothing else to tell anyway. And I'm glad: I feel exhausted after typing these emails. Can't resist any longer – going to doze on the settee for an hour, bye. Audrey.

•

Email From: Stella Bridgeport 09 June 2013 15:53
To: Audrey Ackerman Re: Files on the memory stick

Hello Audrey, hope you're having a pleasant Sunday. I've been in our back garden earlier for weeding and general tidying up. Always say I should do more gardening but never find the time. You like gardening? I remember you mentioning you have a greenhouse. And that you went to the county show last year, coming home with both arms full of pot plants :)

Thanks again for your emails. Please don't think I ignored anything. To explain, I like crime thrillers, and my dramas. Occasionally a romcom. But can safely say I've never read a science fiction novel. And by the sound of it, neither have you. But even if I did, this NanoSynth book wouldn't be one I'd like, I'm sure. I suppose I'm curious what happens with those poor robot people though. (Robots? Or synthetic androids made from swarms of tiny computers inside them. Have I got it sort of right, you think?) His novel is imaginative, agreed, if nothing else.

And I've read the books you've self-published. Enjoyed both of them, particularly The Show Dogs of Kantem. You write in a beautiful prose style. Also know nothing you write is fiction. So I see you wouldn't be the type to make things up or trick me. The chimney fireworks sound fun though! Still, after reading your emails about the android receptionist, and more about those two dogs, I'm just not getting it. And I doubt I ever will. My brain just doesn't work like that. It's just not built to take in that kind of information. I'm a bit of an unimaginative stick-in-the-mud. So I can't relate to events sounding like fiction but aren't, do you see. I've tried but none of it registers. Given it my best shot, as they say. I've attempted answers. Now reached an impenetrable wall and can go no further. The only way for me to deal with this is to think of it as a story, full stop. Bring it on-board as a tale which you need to tell. I will read more but I'm taking a step back. (I'll skip those science fiction notes too. Was finding them confusing and laborious). Have you read more of Gideon Hadley's journal files, Audrey? I admit, a type of fascination is building with those ones. And who knows, there might be a revelation amongst them.

Can I ask for confirmation again. Brown dog is tied in the courtyard and you closed bedroom door on the male one? If yes, I'll phone the farmer tomorrow, check there's no more nuisance barking. Then I'll give The One Dog Inn a bell to see if the dogs have been watered and fed.

Right, I best go. Robert's in the shed. He wants to mow the lawns so got to look busier in the garden to support him! Bye for now, Stella

P.S If you could get back to me about the dogs later today, that'll be appreciated.

•

Email From: Audrey Ackerman 09 June 2013 17:25
To: Stella Bridgeport Re: Files 3 attachments

Hello Audrey, I can understand your standpoint. Best to leave it unexplained; that's my firm conclusion now. (I almost went to write "let sleeping dogs lie" but in a way, wouldn't be funny). We could both throw out explanations till the cows come home and still be none the wiser. Soon I'll move on from it. Well, I have to, for my own good. I'm even attempting to look back on my memories as fiction as well. It might make it all less of an upset in the long run. And thanks for reminding me about The Show Dogs of Kantem. As it happens, Kribley Dog Kennels ordered twelve copies a couple of weeks back and I totally forgot about it. I'd better get that organized as soon as I can.

I do feel bad about those dogs despite the upset they've caused me. To answer your questions: the brown dog was still leashed in the courtyard. As for closing the bedroom door onto the other dog – sorry, but I don't recall that I did, being so upset and distraught at the time. Also I don't know if they are being looked after in any way. I feel it's my responsibility again, please let me phone tomorrow. Not too much worry, as long as the voice from the inn isn't synthetic, that's all I hope.

To your question about the files: yes, I have read more, a short while ago. And I'm struggling with those notes for the science fiction novel too, have to admit. Heavy going, especially as he references fictional scientific essays, as well as technical papers and reports, which I gather are going to be included in his story. He explains in detail the ins and outs of a new sub-genre he's calling Sci-Fi Intense. And the plot is getting thick now; descriptions of the nanotechnology becoming sophisticated far beyond expectation: whole bodies being replaced by nanobots, now include the brains. I assume that's where it starts going wrong, as those with SkinSyn Syndrome have been "rewired" and so it's become easy to mind-control them using mainframe computers. That type of thing, I think.

I might as well round up those sci-fi notes: more detailed chapter breakdowns, more plot twists including the reveal as he calls it, in a later chapter. That is: Beck Sammett, who's meant to be the saviour, is actually the secret force behind Quintessence Industries. And far from trying to save everyone (via Ellie McPearson's rewritten SkinMorph code) he has been making matters worse. And so it goes. I suppose it'd make an interesting film as you said. Far-fetched and unreal though, except for that receptionist at the inn, appearing to be what he describes as science fiction. Or did she have slick makeup and clever acting? But for what purpose? Why would she act out a part as an android? Were there hidden cameras to film my reaction? What for? I'm off again, going round in circles. So I won't mention her any more from now on.

I phoned Dennis to ask if there was a way of cutting out the book notes from pdf files to leave the journal entries only. I tried not to fib when he started asking too many questions; think I got away with it without giving away too much. Did have to say the files were fiction notes, (all of them, journal included) in case he started reading any. He accepted that. Then he told me (to my surprise) there IS a way to amend pdfs (Dennis is much more computer-savvy than I'll ever be). I put the files into an email and sent them over; a couple of hours later he sent them back minus Gideon Hadley's notes for his science fiction book.

Here then are more files, just the journal as mentioned. Gideon is not a happy bunny; his wife Nicole seems to be playing him like a fiddle. Sorry, won't spoil it for you… (You see, I AM beginning to believe these are fiction too; surely a good sign). Best regards, Audrey

•

Email From: Stella Bridgeport 09 June 2013 19:36
To: Audrey Ackerman Re: Files on the memory stick

Hello Audrey. Please, I'll phone Cabbit's Farm and the inn tomorrow, leave it with me. No worrying. And thanks again for more files. Grateful for the novel notes not being there. I'll try reading the others tonight, there's not much on TV. Also Robert doesn't mind me hiding in the spare room for half an hour. In fact, he'll be happy. He can watch his history channel in peace now! Goodnight, take care, from Stella.

*****

Attachment 1 : Journal+NanoS notes 22/5.pdf
Wednesday 22 May 2013 14:15
Journal: In The Tree Bark Snug there's a blood orange-dyed candle – diameter of a side dish – under a glass cover, on a rough hewn shelf that's inset into a flint wall. I'm seated in a fine wingback chair, in front of a fire that's snapping in a splendid fireplace. I've read from a brochure: no matter the season, The Tree Bark Snug never gets warm. Most guests

tend to ignore the snug for that reason. (There aren't any windows and even the radiators make no difference; blazing logs just about take the chill off). So I'm tapping on the laptop in front of their fire in the middle of May, having to push my back into a chair to avoid chilly fingers playing with my spine. At least there's the advantage I'm alone to get on with my journal writing, the conversations from the bar next door sounding no worse than a murmuring stream. And with another glass of red on a copper table beside me, and lunch eaten earlier comforting my stomach, I couldn't ask for much more.

Nicole complained of a migraine and so decided to lay down in the room. Only minutes before telling me she was going up, she seemed well enough although did fire her usual volley of questions. And this was after my attempts to instigate a decent conversation. With her interrogation, it all became a stalemate with no real discussion started. But then, no change there. Staying at the inn for another ten days; hopefully she'll open up later without skirting around our concerns.

At least I should cauterize the two questions I hear from her time and again: "Do you still find me attractive?" and "Why are you always writing your journal?" as though she has never understood the simplest of previous answers. How many more times will I be forced to go into lengthy discourse concerning how beautiful she is and always has been to me; and saying for the umpteenth time concerning my journal: "It's like thinking on paper; it helps exercise writing muscles, and leads to more successful notes for the novels." I'm surprised my creative output hasn't been compromised with having to justify myself so often. How much more does she need to be convinced: if I miss the looming deadline for NanoSynthetica, it could jeopardize people, including myself – my career even?

Am I being selfish? Yet how many times have I analysed that, attempted to unpick it.

A psychologist once gave an unreliable prognosis: that I displayed a few sociopathic tendencies, mainly a lack of empathy with others. Rubbish, of course. Although I guess after twenty-two years with Nicole, compromise can lead to some selfish features otherwise one would swallow the other and suck out personality.

Impressed with breakfast this morning. Smoked bacon and local farm eggs, decent tea and enough toast for an army (but only enough milk for one person – still, a tiny minus). Had a decent window table overlooking a garden area set with box hedges, the bright morning's sunbeams over us.

Nicole seemed happier than usual, smiling and nodding to guests as they walked past. Not a sullen word between us; general chatter concerning the inn and ideas of where we should go in the afternoon. I suggested Gapland Castle as worth a visit, as well as Cloisters of the Attendant Gods heritage site. Nicole didn't seem too keen on either but appeared more enthusiastic about a trip to Stokesflown, for a wander beside the beach; even seemed to consider catching the play at the pavilion. In the end, we agreed it was going to be too hot a day for going out and about, so decided to have a more relaxing time inside. A jazz quartet is playing later in one of the bars; should be worth a listen.

After breakfast we sat in one of the beer gardens with sounds of chittering sparrows and smell of baked bread from the inn's small bakery beside the kitchens. All very nice; calm before the storm. We kept out of the sunshine under a sprawling umbrella, with a pot of tea for two on a wrought iron table, a mass of tulips smothering an old cartwheel beside us. Already a hot start to the day, the temperature more usual for a strong-rayed August afternoon than a morning in May.

I finally broached a more serious subject, our daughter's welfare in her flat – at least, more serious as far as Nicole is concerned. That's what triggered the sudden descent into argument. Nicole always goes on that I never seem concerned about our daughter's welfare – so I thought it best to ask how things were going for Amelie. That's all, a simple, innocuous question. But Nicole became annoyed, telling me I ought to know.

How can I possibly know if Amelie never contacts me? She communicates with her mother now, and still I don't know why she has twisted Amelie's mind to ignore her own father.

Nicole upsets me on purpose. She continued ramping her annoyance, especially when I suggested sending more money to Amelie to help pay her rent. Barrage of abuse started: how I never listen, never consider other people's feelings (whatever that means); how I think problems can be solved by throwing money at them, etc., etc.

I must get this down before I forget: how, as I watched Nicole rant, I was able to tune out her distressed voice as easily as adjusting a volume control. Sitting relaxed in the pleasant heat and defined shadows of the beer garden, surrounded by overflowing flower pots, bumblebees humming about flower heads and trickling tones of the garden's fountain, it became an enchanted haven. Nicole's lipsticked mouth firm, eyes narrowing or flashing, brow creasing then not, her beautiful face animated; arms gesticulating as if a painter giving artistic flourishes to an invisible canvas, then brushing a petal from her cleavage which had floated down from a flower basket. How I love her appearance. She attracted me in an instant with those features of a starlet twenty-three years ago and here, still emanating beauty and exuding irresistible attraction. Yes, I love her for her beauty. Do I still love her for her mind? Or if I lapsed into poetic concepts, her soul? Perhaps not, anymore. Does that matter? Not sure it does – despite the differences and our petty squabbles, we're meant to be together, comfortable in each other's company in the main; we need each other. Maybe for different reasons but that can't be a worry. What can be a concern are the arguments weakening bonds. And perpetuating rumours that she needs comfort from another man is harmful. Part of what needs to be repaired, while here at the inn.

Despite switching off in the beer garden this morning, I seemed to satisfy her worries for a while – she shrugged, and said she was going for a walk through the herb garden. I replied I'll leave her to it and catch up with more notes for the novel. Just before she walked through a gate she turned back to say: "Not going to ask?" I was puzzled and no less so when she added, "Don't forget sunblock?" Still don't know what she meant. (I had a similar confusion concerning a guest passing the breakfast table earlier. He fixed his eyes onto mine, and said, "Sincerity oozes from every pore." I glanced at Nicole with puzzlement but she was gazing out of the window to a thrush, in a birdbath, as it dipped its head and flicked water in a fanned spray from its tail. I'm certain that the man who made this comment and the jogger are one and the same person).

Around half-twelve, Nicole appeared again; and to my joking remark of "That was a long walk in the garden!" she almost bit my head off. I ignored her words and talked her into having a spot of lunch. The sun was over the yardarm so a decent lunchtime drink was in order too.

The crab salad was rather fine. Nicole nibbled at one of her sandwiches and seemed distant, not even bothering much with her drink until I tripped up again. What lit the touchpaper this time, I can't remember; after it initiated rapid-fire questioning, followed by her announcement of a migraine before disappearing upstairs to lie down for a while, I considered I deserved another glass of wine.

Attachment 2 : Journal+NanoS notes 22/5.pdf
Wednesday 22 May 2013 19.38
Journal: Writing can heal the pain, help resolve problems after laying them bare onto the page. I have to type, not only for the benefit of creative writing, but also to repair hurt. Then able to place it at the periphery of my senses, either for it to melt away or be forgotten. Or at best, for it to be solved on its own by a change of circumstances.

That's what I must do in this case: place one word after another into the journal to assist in sanitizing the most recent emotional upsets.

And who else could it be to cause this upset but Nicole. I'm at a loss as to what I've done wrong. I have brought her down to Legatemead to stay in a terrific old inn, prepared to restore our relationship, discuss, erase doubts, cure reservations; help our daughter financially, promises to phone her to attempt reconciliation, discover how I've upset her as well. But after all that, still it's not good enough. What else but move it away for the while, to a mental drawer until the hurt goes? If that's not done and I can't see any solution in the meantime, I'll only be upset. And I can't afford that. I've important work to finish.

Let's list all of Nicole's excuses yesterday and today: tiredness, a migraine, and now after dinner, not wanting to listen to a jazz band. She knows how much I love jazz and still she wouldn't keep me company for a few hours. Surely listening to jazz can't be that much of a miserable experience she made it out to be. So, again we're apart, different places in this rambling building (supposedly haunted), myself seated for a second time in The Tree Bark Snug. I'll be visiting the entertainment room – Gown and Moonlight Bar – in twenty minutes, have a listen to the saxophonist's intricate melodies and the trumpet wailing.

Another mental drawer opened of its own accord. That's the danger of treading water over emotive threads of thought, as I always warn myself. The memory (over twenty years ago for crying out loud) when Nicole threatened to walk out, to leave me on my own, go back to her parents; all because of the disagreement over our then unborn daughter.

We hadn't been together long. It's all here, stored away, ready to be inspected at any time: how she couldn't figure out that returning to her barrister training after giving birth would have been out of order even three years after, as she suggested. The selfishness of that is still fresh and the memory of her slapping my face when I told her as much. I can't remember how I talked her around to staying then, but do recall us not speaking for at least a couple of days. I didn't have time for all of that emotional baggage and still don't. Erase the miserable memory. Best way, otherwise it'll fester then grow out of all proportion.

And now, trying to repair again, not only does she seem to be making efforts to avoid me but also has announced she wishes to impart information at the breakfast table tomorrow. And that I'm not going to like what I hear. I can't be bothered to work out what she means. I'll wait until the morning. But before that time, I'm going to drink a few decent pints and listen to the jazz quintet in The Gown and Moonlight Bar.

Attachment 3 : Journal+NanoS notes 22/5.pdf
Wednesday 22 May 2013 23.46
Journal: Back in this handsome four-poster, blanket over me and the laptop balancing on my knees.

I left the jazz band still in full flow; much atmosphere and ambience, as well as applause, and though the room was half full, the audience vigour made up for it with their warmest of vibes. Talking of which, I have much warm vibes myself from three pints (or was it four?) of their very fine Thunderclap.

Nicole is now asleep beside me. When I came into the bedroom twenty minutes ago, the bed was empty; she appeared a few minutes after I did, clutching sugar and milk rations. She'd only just got them from reception a minute before, she told me. But how could we have missed each other when passing reception at the same time?

Don't know if that made any sense. Typing and ale don't go together. Should have learned that long ago.

Same as trying to hold a decent conversation: I insisted

Nicole told me next morning's information but my slurred comment didn't register with her. Or she chose to ignore my words. Suppose I'll wait until breakfast – bound to be underwhelming.

Really can't think straight. Time for sleep now before I collapse over the laptop. Goodnight me.

•

Email From: Audrey Ackerman 10 June 2013 10:18
To: Stella Bridgeport Gideon Hadley's files

Stella: HE'S FOUND A SECRET DOOR! Speak later.

•

Email From: Audrey Ackerman 10 June 2013 12.53
To: Stella Bridgeport Secret door 2 attachments

You just won't believe what he writes after he goes through the secret door and to the bottom of some stone steps (where there's another door). And guess where that second door leads to—you can, I reckon, if you think about it. But you'll never guess, not even in a million years, what happens after. I'm saying no more. Read the files, Stella, they can only be described as sensational! BFN, Audrey

•

Email From: Stella Bridgeport 10 June 2013 13:15
To: Audrey Ackerman Re: Secret door

Hello Audrey, I don't often check personal emails during a

lunch break, as you know. As you also know, I rarely have a proper lunch hour anyway. Still in a slight rush so I'll try to be brief.

Just read your last two emails. Thought there weren't any more notes for novels? Secret passages have the flavour of adventure books. Won't be reading your attachments till this evening (Robert's taking me out for dinner at French Sam's). But promise I won't forget when I get back.

Inevitable, isn't it. Suzie's just come in and wants me over at D kennels. Have a good day, Stella.

*****

Attachment 1 : Journal+NanoS notes 23/5.pdf
Thursday 23 May 2013 11:09
Journal: I'm spitting fur balls. Nicole has slashed at my heart and isn't the slightest bit repentant. Almost dizzy with the horrible revelation laid on me at breakfast. Once it had sunk in I walked away, leaving her at the table. I'm still furious that she kept such information from me. It reeks of a disrespect for me, her husband, the father of her child.

She could have waited until I'd swallowed that mouthful of fried tomato – I almost choked. For the past year, I've been led to believe that Amelie lives quite happily in a flat in Russex, when in fact for most of that time she's been living with Nicole's father? And to cap that, Nicole tells me she's told me before but it's "never registered"?

I'm shaking right now. But at least it's clear why Amelie hasn't been contacting me, now I know the truth: that her grandfather, my excuse of a father-in-law, has twisted her young mind against me for certain. This is all of Nicole's doing and I'm not sure of the reasons.

That grandfather clock standing in the corner of the bar is taunting. Ticks getting louder, becoming a distraction, almost mocking me in my shocked sadness. I'll take a walk, get some air. No, I'll get a pint first – hair of the dog and all that.

Attachment 2 : Journal 23/5.pdf
Thursday 23 May 2013 18.52
Journal: Now I shake for a different reason. I find myself staring at the fireplace as if I'm able to catch it changing back to its previous state, to prove I've been hallucinating, perhaps due to psychotropic properties in the ale's yeast. But still the side of the secret door is gaping like a missing tooth in the mouth of the fireplace, proof enough for me that the unbelievable experiences actually did happen.

I have to guarantee every detail is recorded for future reference. I'll start from midday today. I must have walked three miles around the grounds, circling the inn at least four times, my mind still in turmoil concerning Nicole's words to me at breakfast.

After an hour of walking, I sat under one of the pergolas for five minutes to empty my head further of wounding memories. And that's when I spied Nicole, appearing to be conversing with the jogger, both of them standing on a gravel path leading to the lake. I called out; not certain she heard but either way, she turned from him and began walking towards me. When I called again, she appeared surprised, stopped and looked back to the jogger who was, by this time, running towards the side of the inn. I stood and went over to Nicole and asked what he wanted. She answered that he needed directions to the boathouse. I did think he must have found that boathouse by now, considering how much he ran around the place.

I convinced her that we should clear the air concerning Amelie. She diverted the conversation to other matters, very neatly may I say, but then I needed to forget anyhow.

I suggested we should have lunch. We walked back to one of the bars. After a beef and mustard sandwich, I came over feeling weary. Pathetic, really, a slow stroll for an hour or so in the warm air and it knocked me out. My turn to have an afternoon nap; I left Nicole sitting on a couch with her gin and tonic, and went up to the room.

I awoke with a start – at about half four – when the latch rattled and the heavy bedroom door swung open with its whine. Nicole had returned; to change for dinner, I guess. In no mood for any argument, I avoided more discussion concerning Amelie. That left only stilted conversation but I persevered. And while I was in the bathroom preparing for a shower, I tried my best to soften the situation with light-hearted remarks thrown through the bathroom doorway, to Nicole in the bedroom. I babbled on too much perhaps, thinking she was listening and passing off my comments as idle chat. That was until I poked my head around the doorframe. I had been talking to myself: Nicole was no longer there. I shrugged and took my shower.

After dressing, I switched the kettle on in the room. As I was about to add milk to the teacup – just after the kettle had boiled – Nicole entered the bedroom again.

I'd commented thirty minutes earlier about a pair of my trousers taken from the suitcase as being creased. I wasn't finding fault, simply pointing out a fact. It was obvious then that Nicole had taken exception to the remark: she had fetched an iron. She put it on a chair seat, went to one of the wardrobes and extracted an ironing board, and unfolded it, standing it at one side of the fireplace. And to my innocent enquiry of, "What's that for?" Nicole snapped something about having to iron my clothes even though the creases in the trousers were due to my bad packing. I couldn't get what the fuss was about.

She went to pick up the iron from the chair but I reached it first. She tried to pull it from my hands with her grip surprisingly strong. I relented and let go. Nicole wasn't prepared for that, I guess; she toppled backwards, the iron flying through the air from her hand, and it struck one of the tiles surrounding the fireplace. The iron had come to rest beside the vase of dried flowers in the hearth.

Nicole was now sitting on the carpet, having fallen there. I extended a hand to help her up but she pushed it away, got to her feet, hot tears in her eyes, and she ranted with a stream of abuse. Frustration, I guess, but to my mind she was overplaying it. I could barely understand what she was saying. I did glean enough to know she was off to visit someone called Maurice.

Maurice? Who the hell is Maurice? I must have said that; didn't receive any answer; she flung the heavy bedroom door open in a rage and rushed out. I sat on the edge of the bed with exasperation, not figuring out how such an innocent remark of mine could have escalated out of all proportion.

Then, after a minute, I left the bedroom and went downstairs to find her.

I looked in a few of the bars and one of the snugs but couldn't see her anywhere. I checked in the beer garden, finally deciding to ask at reception.

The receptionist was the same slick, frosty woman in her starched uniform who had given me such a poor greeting when we had arrived. And to my enquiry, "Have you seen my wife?" her reply of: "Don't know who you mean…sir" was accompanied by a sniff and a narrowing of her heavily made-up eyes. When I mentioned the name Maurice she turned her rigid face from me with a snort. I backed away with slight disgust at the impolite, unhelpful attitude, leaving her to adjust leaflets in the plastic holder, or go from computer to printer with her superior expression, obviously performing any task so as to avoid eye contact.

Realizing my nerves were jangling, I thought a scotch and ginger would do the trick to calm me; but decided I'd pushed the boat out a bit too often since being at the inn and went straight back to the room.

Nicole hadn't returned to the bedroom, or if she had, she had gone again. I poured the cold cup of tea down the bathroom sink. And when back in the bedroom, I folded up the ironing board and put it back in the wardrobe, then went to pick up the iron.

On both sides of the fireplace mantel is a column made of carved wooden tiles, flush with the marble, each with yellow ornamental swirls and purple leaf patterns. I noticed that where the iron had struck, it had damaged one of them. Or at least, that's what I thought at the time. Upon closer inspection, it seemed to have done no more than depress the tile, pushing it inwards by a centimetre. I traced the edge of the depression with my fingers and then noticed that the leaf and swirl pattern had a circle carved in its centre, painted orange. Only then did I see the other tiles had different letters of the alphabet in their middles. I deduced that the circle on the depressed tile wasn't a circle at all but the capital letter "O".

I became intrigued; after fetching a notepad from the writing desk I wrote down the letters from all the 34 tiles. And when sorted into alphabetical order, produced a list: A, A, B, B, C, C, D, E, F, F, G, H, H, K, K, L, L, M, M, N, O, O, P, P, R, R, S, S, T, T, W, W and Y, Y.

When seated at the writing desk, I juggled the letters for a few minutes or so, considering they might make up a phrase, perhaps along the lines of those found carved in the beams downstairs. But it soon became evident that there weren't enough vowels, the only ones being an "O" times two and an "E". I was struck by the fact that the majority of the letters were doubled with the few shown singly. Writing just those single letters down, gave me D, E, G and N. For the reason that the tile with an "O" had first been pushed in, I included that too, adding the second "O" as well. This left me with D, E, G, N, O and O.

I found my solution almost immediately, the anagram too easy to unscramble to make: ONE DOG. A surge of excitement began coursing through my veins. If the first letter of the two words was already depressed, I assumed the other letters could be depressed in order, although I couldn't think of a purpose.

I pushed onto the middle of the wooden tile showing the painted letter "N" and was surprised at how easy it was to move. It slid smoothly inward with a wooden-sounding clunk. It was somehow satisfying and even more so as I continued to press the other tiles, all the way to the second "O", each time that clunking noise as if made by a wooden mallet hitting a clave.

A pause before my index finger moved towards that last tile – upper middle left of the right set – with the letter "G" carved artistically into it. And another pause while the pad of my finger hovered half an inch away. Not with fright, or worry, just a type of relish, anticipation building to a peak until, with a firm push on that last tile, it too moved in. This time, the distinct noise of a locking or unlocking, as if a barrel had rotated and a spring activated from within the firebox area of the fireplace.

I lifted the vase with its dry flowers out of the way and was disappointed at first as it seemed there was nothing worth seeing. But then I noticed a soot-streaked brass panel at the back, at an angle. I instinctively reached for it and pushed. As expected, it made the black gap on its right wider still: it was hinged.

I considered that my legs were beginning to ache from crouching. A moment later, the handle of the bedroom door rattled, the door opening quickly, then Nicole bustled in, looking unhappy.

Standing as quickly as I could, I attempted to shield the lettered tiles with my arms out. Presumably with guilty features because Nicole said, "You look like you're trying to hide something." I insisted that wasn't the case and bent over to pick up the iron from the granite hearth, then returned it to a chest cupboard, in an attempt to draw Nicole's sight away from the fireplace. And while I did that, Nicole launched into a tirade. I admit, most of what she shouted went in one ear and out the other. I was too excited, like an archaeologist might be or adventurer in an ancient city who has discovered a key to unlock a mystery.

I did attempt to pay attention when Nicole mentioned Maurice. And although I expected the worst from her lips, still the hidden panel had overtaken my thoughts and in a way it didn't matter what she was saying. I accepted her rambling explanation, that Maurice is the clumsy jogger often seen chugging around the perimeter of the inn (as if I hadn't already guessed). They spoke to each other, she admitted, and even shared a drink while I was in the snug yesterday. I'm not a jealous type; I halted the speech by convincing her there were no problems, that she deserves friends, even temporary ones. Nicole seemed worried after and explained she needed air, having come over feeling claustrophobic. She walked out of the bedroom as though to prevent herself from speaking further. I called to ask if she wanted me to accompany her. I knew she would say no and that she'd rather be on her own – that suited me: I needed to get back to the secret panel.

I could hear Nicole walking down the bare wooden staircase. I ran to the bedroom door, opened it, and shouted down, 'A long shot but you didn't happen to pack a small torch of any kind, did you?'

If she did hear, she chose to ignore me.

I went back to the secret panel and pushed on it more. And putting my head into the fireplace I could just about make out that it was at least five feet high, now a fair way open at the back of that chimney.

So it was not a panel but a door. I almost pulled a muscle in my back while crawling into the chimney area. And once in, was able to stand straighter with the top of my head into that blackness that the door was revealing. I needed a reliable light source if I was to investigate any further.

When downstairs, I didn't even glance at the reception desk in case the aloof receptionist was there, and walked into one of the bars. There I discovered Nicole sitting on a red leather settee with a glass of white wine in her hand. Her eyes flicked to the bar serving area; I looked over and saw a tall man with his back to me, ordering a drink. I'm certain it was the jogger, Maurice. I turned my attention back to Nicole, her fresh complexion flushed, eyelids fluttering with embarrassment. I shrugged and informed her that I needed to write more notes so wouldn't be accompanying her to dinner in an hour. She didn't seem too worried and accepted my lie with a shrug.

I went to The Candlelit Snug. Despite the stares of a few people there, I picked out one of the candles from its glass holder on a barrel. Nipped the flame out, and headed back to the bar – bidding Nicole farewell for a few hours – into the reception and then on to the stairwell, and up the stairs to the room. All the while I tried to contain my excitement, fingering the tin box of cigarillos with a lighter I'd put inside, both bought the night before. I attempted to keep my heart from beating too fast as I reached the room door, unlocked it and went in.

The vase was still at one end of the hearth and the secret door still ajar inside that chimney breast. After lighting the candle, then with it held out in one hand, I crouched, half crawling into the fireplace. I pushed on the door's side more to open it wider. Raising myself up with my back half bent, I took a step through the door gap and was able to stand upright.

I was in a stone corridor. The walls were made of granite blocks or similar; off to the right, the start of stone stairs. Still with no fright, simmering with intense curiosity, I carefully descended those eleven or twelve steps. I came to an area at the bottom no more than the floor space of seven or eight wardrobes. Three of the walls there were streaked with beams. And these were scratched and carved with lettering and motifs, and unusual symbols. On the fourth wall was a door made of dark wood. Set within it appeared to be the open tops of bottles. I took a step back and by the light of the candle, saw they made patterns. As far as I could make out, it was a stylized representation of an animal's head, more than likely that of a dog. And as yellow light flickered across it, I noticed two things: the representation of the dog's eyes were made from a few red and black glassed bottle ends. And that there were phrases scratched into the wood around the bottle end patterns. I read the ancient graffiti out loud: "No ceremony, can turn back", "No preparation to help" and "Goodbye to what you think you know", before deciding to write them down. So I placed the candle on a horizontal wall beam jutting out enough to make a ledge, and scribbled those phrases into my notebook. I didn't know what to make of them. I was still keen to continue my unexpected adventure and without a second thought, pushed on the door. It didn't budge – it was held solidly shut.

My disappointment didn't last long though, for bringing the candle lower, I discovered a duplicate set of tiles to those both sides of the fireplace. A thought came to mind that the first set was a way of keeping most people out but this set of tiles shown by the light of my yellow candle flame was to keep someone or something in, akin to a prison cell. I quickly dismissed the idea, my hand trembling with a building excitement of the unknown as I pressed the correct sequence again: ONE DOG. With the pressure upon the final carved tile, there were similar clunking wood and unlatching sounds I had heard previously. Then the whole door split into two, opening a couple of inches as a pair of slim doors. Sunlight showed as a glowing streak between them.

What I am about to type is one of the most – no, THE most extraordinary experience I've had in my life. It's still alive in my head and heart, a burning flame which will never die. How to express in words those unimaginable happenings which have given me elevated consciousness within? I know that no matter how well I recount the events, they will portray only a poor imitation of the actual overwhelming experience.

I blew out the candle flame and put the candle in my pocket. Then I pushed on those two doors: they opened easily. I was temporarily blinded by a bright, late afternoon sun. Shielding my eyes with a palm, I stepped forward and stood on paving slabs. They were embedded with bottles inset into solid stone, each bottle end emanating hazy smears of radiating hues.

The sky was light purple with deep mauve clouds. Total silence. And as my eyes adjusted, I found myself at one end of the inn's courtyard. Or at least, an area similar to the design of the courtyard, almost identical but for a few different features. There were a couple of picnic benches at the sides but no round tables or table umbrellas to be seen, and the cast iron chairs were in a line along the left wall. The hot air was different somehow, seeming to vibrate in an inexplicable way, shafts of green light dissecting the overall mauvish brightness.

Then it happened, the sudden tipping over of my world, a bending and twisting of reality. With ominous rumbling like the beginnings of faraway thunder, I began to see an exceptional sight. Mentioning how I began to see, for this became obvious there was a shift in perspective, changing angles of perception, a lifting of scales from my wide eyes. A new learning how to see beyond. There, running along the righthand whitewashed and lathed wall of the courtyard, was the ghost of a running dog, massive and powerful. The more I stared – my sight locked – the more it gained substance, the phantom-smoke becoming opaque while it changed to bright orange. This was a dream within reality yet more than a dream – even more than a lucid one could ever be. That playing with time and space seemed natural and expected while this entity leapt from the end of the wall onto the next wall at right angles to it (similar to a fairground motorcyclist defying gravity in his cage), its size morphing. First huge then going to small, the speed of it changing from faster than any animal can run, to a type of slow-motion. And all the while, that rumbling, with the sultry May air vibrating with a different frequency, making me elated but also frightened. But as frightened as I became, I was also transfixed, taken over with a type of hypnosis, a fascination for that vision.

The air changed in quality yet again, now seeming to

breathe with an intense energy as if an organism itself. My palms sweated. I became weak at the knees when the rumbling and fiery dog streaked to another wall, then leapt in a spiralling arc to the paving with its head low, belly to the ground. And it's the size of a bull elephant, this dog, creeping as though a stalking lion. My heart missing beats, my feet seeming to have melded with the ground, unable to move even as that creature moved closer over the embedded bottle bases of the damask-veined courtyard. The thought: I am about to be ripped apart.

When one is threatened, there's an inventiveness that comes into play. As part of the survival instinct, the mind finds unexpected resources to cope. It was as though I had known all along where that secret part of me could be found: I stretched out an arm with my sweat-glistening palm facing that creeping beast as I suddenly knew this was enough. It didn't stop it from moving but made it stop increasing in size. There was a reverse perspective, however that can be possible, larger the further away it was yet smaller by comparison the closer it got. So that when the fiery form reached me and crouched on the ground three yards away, it appeared no bigger than a greyhound. Admittedly not a small breed but still much smaller than this creature at first appeared.

I put my arm down to see its eyes set within a squarish head. Irises as glowing black opals, each pupil a pinpoint of orange. My whole view not so much plunged into them as drawn as if by a magnetic force. I feared a dark void would take over and transport me to a cold place. Instead I was given a vibrance of an unexpected frequency. Almost a melody, pure and simple enough to capture my awareness. Then the world became it.

Mild panic gripping my throat: quickly losing identity, being drained of it or willingly giving it away. And as the red dog stands from its crouching position, I need to summon a willed strength to be capable of turning away from its all-encompassing gaze.

The spell broken suddenly when it opens its strong jaws to reveal perfect rows of polished, black teeth. I back away with alarm, slowly stepping so as not to startle it more. Hear growling from it, as if it were speaking sequences of vowels, modulated in almost a sing-song way.

Captivated again, I pause, but force myself to run back to the double doors as fast as I am able. Fling them open, lurch through, pull hard to shut them, blindly feel my way in the darkness to the beginning of the stone steps. Stagger upwards in the velvet black until reaching the top, almost toppling out of the secret door, bent double; out through the fireplace and onto the carpet of the bedroom.

I must have been there for ten minutes or more in a trance of sorts, within a sphere of meditation concerning what I had experienced. Every minute or so, a yearning took hold—to go back, to see those striking eyes, be gladly taken over by the transcendent dog's presence which had given a remarkably skilful performance while emanating true and high intelligence. I had to resist; I must resist.

It's getting close to eight. I didn't realize I'd been typing for so long. I'm going to ignore the fireplace, go down to see if I can find Nicole. What happened next will be easy to put down later: it can never be forgotten – it has become indelible, etched into my memory.

Attachment 3 : Journal 24/5.pdf
Friday 24 May 2013 00.57
Journal: Nicole asleep. Her breathing is gentle with exhaled sighs, accompanied by the pattering of a light rain on those two high windows left and right of the fireplace. I'm staring at the dried flowers vase as if I can see through it. The vase is more than enough to conceal the brass door behind, hidden in shadow. I had pulled shut those two doors onto the courtyard, though left the one in the back of the chimney open. Not understanding how to reset the mechanism I didn't want to spoil any chance of using it again.

A sudden temptation to go down into the secret version of the courtyard – but no, it would be dark, not to mention the rain; I must push the thought out of mind.

Back to those leaded windows high up, it's just dawned on me: of course, they must both overlook the courtyard. I could borrow a stepladder to take a look tomorrow, or even now. The night porter could be helpful. But even if he did lend me a stepladder in the early hours of the morning without any judgement, what could I see through thick diamonds of glass into a heavy blackness?

Still I can't sleep. Woke up fifteen minutes ago, dared to turn on my lamp – a contained yellow glow over my side so considered it shouldn't disturb Nicole. Now a gusting wind added to the rain and the breathing sounds still from her. I'll take another sip of whisky; glad I remembered my hip flask this time.

Does the entity sleep, when reddish dog or not? Either way, the presence is there now, visible via that inter-dimensional portal, the gateway to a hidden realm, with thirty guests snoring in their rooms, blissfully unaware.

Only I have that knowledge. I am privileged to have seen the One Dog; equally privileged to have witnessed the metamorphosis. I have been touched, not just physically, but—how? Emotionally, psychically? It's intangible, this other-worldly being's effect upon my spirit, yet real and unfading, unable to be shifted; I'm inhabited by it now.

How could I have ever predicted what would happen on my second visit? All I knew before then was of meeting a manifested dog that transmitted fluent energies which I can't even begin to describe.

The only way to stop myself plunging back through the fireplace this afternoon was to run out of the bedroom to break the irresistible attraction, down the stairs and out of the nearest door to the grounds. Keep myself walking, clear my buzzing mind, push out memories of it by filling my head with one single mission: find Nicole.

Earlier super-real events had, and has, become the norm. So then the afternoon sky arcing with colourless clouds over the grounds, gloomier ones lining the horizon, and a dull sun, were all disappointing by comparison with the mauve-streaked courtyard and its astonishing inhabitant. Outside appeared as if something intrinsically important was missing from the air, from the landscape, and people as well. Other guests of The One Dog Inn I encountered had featureless blank clods serving as their faces.

After ambling through a herb garden (even that seeming underwhelming) and then over a bland lawn, who should I meet trotting around a corner, towards a pergola clad with withering jasmine, but the jogger in his tracksuit. "Hey, you!"

was all I shouted, meaning to ask if he'd seen Nicole in the grounds. At that, his thick neck and waist revolved, splodge of a face creasing into an unidentifiable expression. And he bellowed the inevitable "Can't stop" before promptly spinning on his heels, (quite admirable, I suppose, as he's a tall and large man) before running in the opposite way he had come.

I went in the direction the jogger was originally running. As I walked under the pergola, around to the side of The One Dog Inn, there was Nicole sitting on a bench next to plant troughs and topiary, reading a paperback. I went over and called her name. She looked up from her reading with surprise. Interesting to note her beautiful visage hadn't changed like the others.

A stunted conversation followed, Nicole seeming distant and preoccupied, myself desperate to revisit the courtyard. There seemed an invisible window between us – unseen but destructive – like a sealed glass pane, preventing any proper communication. I can't recall much of what we spoke about, less than seven hours later. Did I demand she confirm again the identity of the jogger as being Maurice? And tell her once more we wouldn't be sharing the evening together? A vague recollection of Nicole answering a question with another of her random ones: "What was I wearing yesterday?" It was then I succumbed to my new addiction, becoming washed over with the irresistible desire to go back to the courtyard that very minute, the compulsion impossible to ignore. I left Nicole, there on the bench.

Not one memory exists from that moment, up until I stood swaying before those double doors at the bottom of the stone steps, with the candle in my quivering hand. The journey from

Nicole to the entrance could have taken a day or the time it takes to snap two fingers.

The urgent pressing of the tiles in order, the energetic pushing of the double doors, the unhesitating stepping through into the magical version of the inn's courtyard. Immediately a relief, no different than an addicted smoker inhaling smoke for the first time in hours, or the warm satisfaction felt after finishing a brandy. Swaddled in that comforting air with its dappling streaks of green, swarms of yellow specks glittering as they floated in waves, in and out of the clearcut purple shadows – I was sated.

I scanned the decorated wall blocks, the plastered areas, around and about the few tables, raised flower beds and shrub boxes in search of the dog. Captivated by another visual anomaly: like patterns made by reflecting mirrors, wherever I looked was repeated indefinitely at the edges of my vision. If I studied an area of paving, that same arrangement of slabs and stone blocks was duplicated far into the distance. The same with a section of wall, seen to repeat over and again, to make it incredibly long, disappearing over a distant mauve-wreathed horizon.

Then as quickly as a light switch is activated, the mass duplication was no more. Instead, across the ground and walls, I perceived large rodents darting here and there. It was frustrating for when I attempted to catch sight of any single one, then the creature vanished. And all the while, discs of light moved over every surface, no different than that produced by discotheque lighting; this accompanied by a complex noise, a multitude of hollow sounds as if produced by the blowing across of hundreds of bottles ends.

Was this playful visual and aural treat a ruse to calm the senses, made to lull me into a false sense of security? Like a magician's cunning deflection of audience attention, I hadn't noticed those small animals had vanished to leave a single animal. Or, for all I knew, had amalgamated into the one – the fully grown dog with its coat similar to a fox. Though this animal's coat changed to orange and yellow, then back to red again, as if a glowing coal being blown. The dog crouched, as it did before, at the other end of the courtyard. With body low and legs bent, it crawled forward as if furtively or hunting me.

When this mysterious creature was halfway across the courtyard – in the middle of it – my brain became made of glass. There's no other way to describe the feeling. And with the backdrop of a myriad of lights moving, and once more those growled vowel sounds inhabiting my ears, I heard a voice. It said: "Hurt me."

Are we all damaged by sights, events and experiences we should never have had? Either by other people's negative actions, from television or from the internet. All stored away in the unconscious – our own version of RAM – ready to be recalled at any time when the keys to unlock those memories are used? Upon hearing those words, my mind churned through a list of ways a dog could be harmed. I have never ill-treated an animal nor ever would. But still a torrent of shocking and evil ideas came to me from nowhere and I seemed incapable of stopping them. And as if the dog had ability to encompass my thoughts in a telepathic fashion, it appeared startled. It leapt into the air, now the same size as a rhinoceros. As it sailed over me, brushing the top of my head with its belly, it let out a heart-rending howl as if being beaten with a stick.

After it brushed my head, warm pulses fanned through mind and body like a dye blossoming in clouds within liquid. An intense elation, a state of being which I have never encountered before; a unity of mind, body and life force as delightful as a new inspiration. And at the peak of the experience, with sensations no less than the height of an aware ecstasy, I became timeless. I was forever; perfect, whole, indestructible, infinite. I had been lit up.

Was the receding of that ultimate knowing and feeling akin to rolling waves returning to a silvery sea? No such poetry: if it started as that, it ended as mundane an experience as murky water spinning from a bathtub. I was left with poor, distant echoes, a pathetic replica of what I had become. No more than a shell devoid of any real substance, the ultimate truth having finally ebbed away.

Nicole still sleeps. She's acquired dark pads under her eyes. She told me earlier she had been crying though the reasons for her tears didn't register with me.

The rain has stopped. I'm getting weary now but I'll try to finish writing events up to the end of the day, at least.

Here I'll mention again for the small chance others will one day read these entries. For your attention: everything you have read or will read (other than in the sections marked Notes) are facts, or at least what I remembered to be factual. Although I'm a writer of fiction, all of my journal entries are based on truth. If you don't trust me or believe what I write, what more can I say?

Back to the dog: the elated filling then emptying of my soul in the courtyard left me with such disappointment as to bring tears to my eyes.

Not for long though. Another visual treat began, enough for me to forget myself. As the animal leapt up to a wall and once again ran sideways at full pelt, it changed speed as before. From ridiculously fast to slow – as if a slowed-down film. And I noticed its front paws weren't making contact with the surfaces of the walls at any point of the run cycle. More than that, it appeared to be rearing up, to run on its back legs like a circus animal act. Then an astounding thing occurred: the animal form, that of the flaming dog, was changing into a human being before my amazed sight. Eventually to leave a fully formed figure, dressed in an orange cowl and cloak, much like a medieval monk might have worn. And still defying gravity along a right-hand wall, trotted sideways towards me at a fast pace.

Now I can't keep eyelids from closing; they're smarting. The next part of what happened in the courtyard yesterday afternoon will have to wait. Still, despite that, and even though it's getting on for two in the morning, I feel the urge to go downstairs, ask the porter for more milk cartons or coffee sachets, any excuse to walk back to the room via those courtyard's windows, to inspect its moonlit interior for cast shadow, human shadow, fleeting shadow, moon-tinged shadow, dog shadow. But I will resist, I must. I'll save this, shut the laptop, switch off the light, and get some sleep before I make myself ill.

*****

Email From: Stella Bridgeport 10 June 2013 19:45
To: Audrey Ackerman Re: Secret door

Dear Audrey, Robert printed out the files you sent. Don't worry, I know he didn't read any. For all he knows, they're documents from the Centre. Finished reading them in the conservatory not long ago. Do you know, I quite enjoyed it! Don't mind if you send more. Puzzle tiles, secret doors, fantasy courtyard, the One Dog transforming into a monk. What imagination this Gideon Hadley has! I never thought I'd be gripped by such a story, but I have been. Maybe I'll start reading more fantastical books. And find patience with the special effects films from now on. :)

But can I take on board all about the wavering relationship with Nicole, and the jogger named Maurice, as being real? I think so, that seems believable. It's real life, like a drama based on reality, normal events and so forth. Right, pizza is here soon. Not often we have a home delivery. Better go. Regards, Stella

•

Email From: Audrey Ackerman 11 June 2013 14:27
To: Stella Bridgeport Re: Secret door 2 attachments

Dear Stella, to think that over the course of two weeks I've considered anti-depressants, visit to a psychiatrist, and running away. I worked through ideas that I might have been developing a brain disease, ranging from a minor neurological condition all the way to a dreadful tumour. I've been tearful, listless, snappy, an insomniac, sleepy, angry, sad. There's probably a few more emotional states I've forgotten as well. And all this from a single visit to The One Dog Inn on Wednesday 29th last month. Even though I've appeared happier last week up until yesterday, the truth is I've been hiding a lot of what I've been feeling. You could say I became calmer only because of an inability to deal with my distressing experiences, all shuffled away. Out of sight, out of mind. With problems not dealt with, I still felt much stress, almost without knowing it. (Does that make sense?)

But I'm stressed no longer, or sad or snappy, or any of the rest. I'm refreshed and back to my old self. This morning I arranged a trip to Greenwaters Shopping Mall for next week with Gloria (you can come along as well, if you like) and spoke to Dennis on the phone for at least an hour. Even laughed along to his silly jokes; and we sorted much. He still doesn't know what's been going on but I filled in a few details, enough to allay worries he had, without giving too much away. Don't mean to keep secrets from him (that's not good in any relationship, is it). He will know the full story one day, and now perhaps sooner than I would have thought. So why is that? And why am I calm and collected with much dynamism and energy returning? One reason: I have now read all of those files from the memory stick. Be my guest, Stella, to continue thinking it's been made up, even the romantic story of Gideon, Nicole and Maurice, if you decide. It really doesn't matter a single jot if you don't believe, Robert doesn't believe, anyone else doesn't believe.

Whether fiction or non-fiction, nightmare or dream, whatever, the last of those files provided all the jigsaw puzzle pieces, now locked into place for a perfect explanation. Everything is fully understood as to what and why I heard and saw.

Dennis is attending a conference over in Banchester early next month (his colleague Roland will hold the fort at the pharmacy while he's away) and he's asked me to go with him … he'll pay hotel expenses, the lot (told Dennis I can't let him do that but after ten minutes of his insistence, I gave up arguing). I've decided we will go away together. He's pushing our relationship forward faster than I'm used to with other boyfriends (don't believe I've just typed that word!) but then I'm not exactly a spring chicken, am I…(don't answer that ;)

The conference is held over a week. If I were to come back to the Centre at the beginning of next week as I'd planned, I'd only be available for two weeks before I went again. That's not fair on you, Stella, especially as I've been gone for almost three weeks already. So I think the right course of action for me is to resign. You've been mucked around for long enough.

Right, time I did the vacuuming; I'll leave it there. The final files are attached, as requested. Even reading them as fantastic fiction, it's still mind-blowing. (Isn't that what they used to say in the 60s? :) Best regards, Audrey

P.S Hope you and Robert enjoyed your pizza yesterday; and before I forget, a correction for you: the dog doesn't transform into a monk. You'll see.

*****

Attachment 1 : Journal 24/5.pdf
Friday 24 May 2013 08.32
Journal: Nicole can't have been bothered to wake me up, and gone downstairs on her own again. Don't know what's gotten into her; we're here to cement our relationship. Beginning to have doubts that'll happen.

I'll miss breakfast and carry on the journal from where I left off at half one this morning, then to finish with the revelation which came to me twenty minutes ago.

As if I need reminding: I'm fond of special effects. I've seen some staggering ones over recent years, the most enduring tricks of the eye found in cinema, of course, produced by using camera angles, makeup techniques, perhaps combined with stop-motion, computer graphics, etc. But no matter how proficient film effects can be, still they're 2D; virtual, locked into the celluloid or tape, or made from digital bits. There's no way for them to be seen within the three-dimensional world. Then what if they could be, those transformations viewed in real space? The entertainment industry would explode in popularity anew. Imagine people's reactions to jaw-dropping scenes played before them – more vivid, more solid-looking than any hologram, indistinguishable from a physical object, right there in the middle of their living room. They would be elevated with utmost awe, no different than how awe-struck I was while watching the remarkable dog becoming 3D, quickly changing into a solid hooded figure.

But even that was no match for what happened next. Again I must somehow translate the next experience into words, beginning with the monk's somersault from the wall, to land on his feet on the courtyard ground. Head down so that the cowl cast a shadow on the face, still a hidden identity. I might have asked, "Who are you?" I'm not certain I did; either way, slim hands pulled back the cowl from the head. I stepped back in surprise at what I was seeing: shoulder-length hair – the tone of copper – strands as thick as cables, twisted in plaits and twirls, gently coiling and uncoiling, serpent-like, the face seeming to be made from light brown twigs constantly moving, both hair and face components becoming thinner but multiplying with an organic resolution. Finer and finer the elements became, until the face glowed with an aura, skin as smooth as a pebble; those features belonging not to a man but to a young woman. Still those glowing orange points in black eyes, subtle smile upon moistened lips, her mouth opening as if about to speak, but no words spoken.

I trembled at her beauty and although I studied that female of average height before me with fascination, there was the sense she towered above everything, a hundred feet high, a giantess, a supernova deprived of substance relating to darkness, a luminous divine light, an energy-emanating goddess.

Did I experience a whirl of events or a casual playing-out in this young woman's company? Seconds became minutes then hours, then milliseconds. In her domain, encapsulated and hidden from everyday life, time had no relevance. With prismatic patterns swirling behind her, sliced through with those green shafts, instinctively I knew instruction had begun – my first lesson.

She transformed back to her dog identity and ran along the walls, which had become bookcases heaving with leather-bound volumes. She stopped at random, turning to me, speaking in a foreign tongue, her dog voice thick and guttural, before moving on to the next book until, in between the spines of two white books, she pointed with a paw to the open neck end of a dark blue bottle near the ground. I walked towards it: the closer I got, the larger the neck opening became so that when I was close enough to look into it, the glass tube swallowed my head and shoulders. I found myself peering into a telescope of sorts, espying a busy medieval town with tradesmen in their smocks going about their business between the alleys of Gothic houses lined with clay pots; sounds of a market throng, plucked strings of a lute; carts and horses, hay bales, a flock of geese, women selling apples and root vegetables.

Then I was taught to construct anything I could think of – reality carving it could be called – objects made from particles of nothing: planets the size of weather balloons hovering two feet from the ground; geometric shapes made to revolve and lock together; other formations and structures to move along tracks; ability to amend or change them into anything else at any speed and imbue them with texture; have them vanish when finished with, as easily as clicking on the delete button in a computer program. The processes were the overlapping of newly-created, vivid worlds within hyperreality. Next I was given abilities to create sound multitudes without instruments, instigate ancient voices, invoke speeches using dialects of many nations. Then learning to communicate with her via a form of telepathy. My mind became spiritually oiled, working as expertly as any philosopher's, as relentlessly as pistons of a massive steam engine; until finally she told me her name, with a startling revelation revealed to me that I'd always known her name — Lilah.

Within her metaphysical presence I escape any future containing stagnation. She seduces with innocent charms, this beautiful creation who expresses with a becoming fragility, who vibrates the blood in my veins. I look to her and comprehend the principles of desire, the fundamental basis of all love.

And then I found myself laying on the four-poster bed unaware of how I got there, the dark mahogany panels of its ceiling coming into focus, with a dread sensation I'm in a state of virtual, the only true reality to be found in the courtyard. I listened to Nicole breathing under the covers beside me, and wondered how she could be so real within the unreal.

This morning's light is surprisingly strong from the windows either side of the fireplace but those things have been made simplified. Everything is insubstantial, as if the bedroom has passed through an all-encompassing filter. It could be said that my senses have undergone the same process. Outside the courtyard, away from Lilah, my perceptions are still blunted, washed-out.

Lilah haunts the senses. She's my total preoccupation. The moment I awoke this morning, her fascinating face was the first image to form in my inner eye.

I picked up the laptop from the side of the bed and then Googled all manner of things: phantoms and apparitions, wraiths, angels, gods and goddesses, divine messengers, even demonic personalities, one web link leading me to another until I found, almost by accident, a CycloWik article illuminating the ultimate truth concerning Lilah.

Simply put, she belongs to a rank not far from that of angels, possessing much intelligence, able to appear as a human being, as well as any chosen animal form. Lilah is nothing less than a genie, also known as a djinni.

I've changed my mind. I'll get out of this claustrophobic bed, have a quick splash, then meet Nicole in the breakfast room after all; attempt to play out the day in this poor, lesser dimension.

Attachment 2 : Journal 24/5.pdf
Friday 24 May 2013 20.41
Journal: I had no choice. They deserved it for what they did to me. I must continue to remain unmoved, be without remorse. If only the pitiful howling that echoes from the courtyard would stop though, just for a minute.

Have to keep strong. Surely it should be easier, now that I'm becoming defined and elevated, swamping fog lifting from the machinery of the mind.

I'm in perfect control of my destiny, a discernment of formidable potential within. When put into practice, I'll attain stupendous power ready to unleash. I am prepared; already converted, beginning to transmute, humming like an electrical installation.

For the while I can only influence the local but soon it will be global. When bestowed the keys to the planet's next evolutionary stages, I'll have abilities to transform cities, countries, continents, the whole world. All of that awaits. An inspirational creator, the pioneering, esoteric champion, builder of a positive and miraculous new world order. I will become nothing less than a god.

Will I eventually turn mad with power? If so, I suspect it will be a delicious madness. But I can't see this happening providing there's no underestimation, no feeble taming or weak acceptance. Strength of mind will give me benign control and unquestioned authority, a future filled with magnitude, the utmost generosity and graciousness.

But first the persistent, grating barks have persuaded me. I have to be punished.

Trees wave branches in this chill air. Above, blustering clouds are a single piece of scenery, the whole of it one anonymous image moving across the void. Below, twilight infecting the landscape, making it no more than cold and dark soot, a solidified ash.

Nicole shouldn't have torn our relationship to shreds.

If only she had agreed to come here to be stunned, to gasp in reverential excitement. Hold tightly onto my arm, beg for more miracles while the magnificent giant swans drift closer over shimmering waters of the lake, push through lily pads, to tower above us and glow ivory. Watch them flap their enormous, glorious wings to make gusts of air and bassy whomping sounds as strong and loud as a wind creates on a blustery day.

There needs to be a fine-tuning of these wonders of new nature: I have seen a few attempted flights. But being as my huge swans are still under the control of everyday laws of physics, their speed across the lake isn't fast enough for the massive, plump bodies to lift into the air. Eventually I will have them fly up easily, in formations, even perform in aerobatic ballets.

The sunset is almost complete. The cloud backdrop is no

more, having become a bruise; the pastel moon is gaining definition.

Over by a huddle of dark bushes: a fox, a badger or even a large cat, its eyes glowing from the light of the burnt silver moon rays as brightly as a pair of LED lamps.

Amazing day and a disastrous day. Like the days before, it must be recorded for posterity.

After finishing up typing this morning's notes, I washed and dressed, then made my way down to the breakfast room. No sign of Nicole there. I assumed she had finished and was sitting in one of the bars to read her newspaper.

Not many other guests remaining in the breakfast room so was able to choose a decent table by a window again. I had a healthy appetite. After a waitress brought hot toast in its rack, she took my order of coffee, eggs, bacon and mushrooms.

While waiting for the food to be cooked, there was time to relax, to impress myself with the serenity I felt within a gentle, meditative calm. Easily taken on board I had met a transforming genie; unfazed by it, accepting as if an everyday occurrence. And now I knew her identity, as well as her name, tensions and anxieties had melted away.

There didn't seem to be any particular urgency to revisit her – I had all the time in the world. And I almost laughed out loud when the thought was born: I had also been given the world. For aren't genies – in film, literature, mythology and legend – generous givers of gifts? Make a wish, any wish, to one of these mystical beings and it is brought into reality for you.

Then surges of triumph running through my very bones, electrifying the flesh, as an army of ideas charged my brain.

The obvious ones like becoming a billionaire or acquiring instant fame held little attraction for me and were quickly dismissed when compared with those other visionary, expressive concepts springing forth.

The cooked food arrived. I ate it, my mind still focused on the multitude of potential requests I could make to Lilah.

My section of the breakfast room was now empty of other guests. I assumed it was the same the other side of the stainless steel salad bar which acted as a room divider. That was until I heard the clatter of a knife on a plate, followed by hiccupping sobs from that side, bursting the quietness.

I left the remains of my breakfast and walked around the salad bar to the other side, and sure enough there was Nicole, crying, sitting back with arms folded, head down. Seated opposite her was the jogger – wearing shorts and a striped shirt this time – gesticulating and mumbling. He stopped speaking; Nicole held her hands to her ears. I walked up to them and said quietly, "Aren't you going to introduce me?"

Nicole let out a gasp and Maurice, glancing up, said, "Tell him now." He scrutinized me, appearing concerned, looking me up and down as if he were my doctor and me his patient. And as I asked, "Tell me what?" he stood, the chair legs screeching across the blue slate tiles. Then he wiped his mouth with a napkin before uttering his favourite pair of words, "Can't stop."

"Is that all he says?" I asked Nicole as he strode out of the breakfast room. And then I could have added, "Tell me what, that your new-found friend has become your lover? While I was witness to sublime acts of celestial beauty you were writhing together in your own acts, in bed together?"

Did I mention to her that it didn't matter she was having an affair? I learnt to accept years back when my suspicions were first aroused, I realized; now easy to dismiss. Fine that it was out in the open, as long as she came back to me, stayed with me, loved me; and for her to listen, take in the incredible events of yesterday: tiles and secret doors, the duplicate, overlaid courtyard, a dog that becomes a young woman, who is a djinni, a superhuman creature called Lilah living in that mystical realm, able to grant wishes. This I babbled with enthusiasm, then awaited Nicole's comment, not expecting the one I got. She exploded into a traumatic torrent of tears, a torrent of angry words too, accusing me of being in the grip of a mental illness; then changing her mind, insisting I was lying and that the lies were deceitful and cunning, believing that Lilah was my secret mistress.

I was desperate to prove to Nicole that what I said was true; and in a way, I needed to prove details myself. Up until that point, I had blindly accepted Lilah as being a genie and able to bring into being anything I wished for.

I tried to leave then, to return to the hidden courtyard, but Nicole held onto my arms with her words rushing, choking back tears while she told me her own lie: how she did have an affair, not with Maurice, but with me. What cruel drivel was this? That she hadn't met Maurice for the first time on Tuesday; she has known him even before we met at university; how Maurice had been reduced to pulp by our affair, how his iddy-biddy heart had been broken.

I gave her credit, what a masterful piece of storytelling, an adept turning of the tables. I managed to release myself from her grip. And as I ran out, she screamed for me to return, that the revelation wasn't her confession, and what I needed to be told was going to rip me apart. I thought those words meant nothing, that she was playing games…

Stop the barking and whingeing, please, please.

One of the giant swans has floated right up to the lake edge, looming out of the twilight, towering above me, bending its massive supple neck, the orange beak at least five feet long. It is almost within reaching distance from the bench I'm sitting on. I have no fear; still tapping the laptop keyboard with this monster specimen so huge it's blocking out the light from the moon. It could be as if it's about to peck me. My life would be extinguished by a jab as forceful as being hit by a truck. But I instinctively know it wouldn't harm me. There, it's turning away to move back across the black glass of the lake.

To continue: I wanted, I needed, to visit Lilah.

It didn't take long to be standing back in the courtyard, summoning her. Once more, time became meaningless – I have no recollection of how long I stayed, or how much was communicated, translated, telepathically transmitted. I do recollect though that altering reality to emanate out from within the courtyard confines was as easy for Lilah as a slight tilting of her beautiful head, a stroke of one of her fiery red tresses, or a slow and graceful turning of the wrist, performed with a childlike enthusiasm.

Describing desires I wished to be brought into reality was easy, and even easier after practice with help from Lilah amending my visualized images. And each time this happened I experienced an exhilarating sensation similar to ice-cold water splashes on a sun-heated scalp.

I must have bade her farewell and found myself walking

towards the car parks. And once there, bellowing out the word "Hallelujah!" at the sight of green and red apples, each a perfect specimen, hanging down from every stout branch of the oak trees. A total success: an ultra-designing of reality, a miraculous manipulation of uncountable atoms – similar to how nanotechnology will work – to bring into being the desire of the willer. I buzzed with the potential of it all. This was just the beginning.

Nicole had to see; I promised her. She would be amazed, begin to discern our future in store. We could start fresh from square one again.

But first I needed to see my swans. And after standing at the lake's edge for a good twenty minutes, entranced by their stunning beauty, (as I still am now) I went back inside to search the bars and snugs for Nicole.

Unable to find her anywhere, I made my way out again to the archway and through into the beer garden. Within an enclosed seating area not far from the restaurant, there she was, sitting again and reading her book. She insisted I listen to her; I insisted she put her book down and follow me, so as to see ultimate truths, those first wishes fulfilled, and be amazed by them.

She would not come; would I have to drag her to the apples then the swans? I put my hands under her armpits, pulling upward; she stood as if willing. But when I took hold of her wrists to pull her from out of the beer garden towards the lake path, she shouted and pulled them from my hands, backing away as though frightened. How could she be frightened of me?

Then—any soft landing, an easing in before telling me her

filthy, pathetic rot? No. She came right out and said it, eyes flicking, arms and shoulders shaking as if she was cold, telling me again how she and Maurice were together before I was on the scene; how they lived in Warpington, had a cottage there; how she had started her university course unaware she was pregnant; eventually giving birth to a beautiful baby she called Amelie.

Why did she keep on stabbing me with her savage and callous sentence: "You're not Amelie's father, Maurice is Amelie's father."

I could have collapsed to the ground, bones becoming jelly; maybe I did. I heard a voice – my voice, and I can still hear it taunting, calling from shadows, from out of the stone walls, the cobbles and flagstones, saying they must be punished.

This lie, inhuman filth of a lie; this Maurice, a deceiver, a wife-stealer, a daughter coveter. A dog that has to be beaten, who deserves to suffer. And if he's a dog, Nicole is his bitch from hell.

How long did I reel about? Where did I go, how did I stop the agony of a seething brain, as painful as acid thrown onto it? I've no idea; but what I do know is I'm back by the lake, scanning the black water: giant swans over the other side looking no more than silhouettes of yachts.

The idea was conceived. Turn Nicole into a dog – that's what was needed. Let her feel mental anguish like she'd given me; then teach Maurice a lesson with an imaginative punishment, I thought.

How I lashed out in Lilah's courtyard – gnashing, grinding my teeth – not asking, demanding these transformations, my memory hunting, blaming even the innocent receptionist for being part and parcel of their deceit.

Nicole still howls. I can only blank it out for a short time.

Despairing. It dawned on me an hour or more after leaving Lilah's domain how simply cruel I've become: finding a length of rope, leaping at the petrified Nicole as dog, tying it about her neck and dragging her to the courtyard, wagging a finger like a strict schoolmaster reprimanding a naughty student. Then her cowering and shivering before slinking away behind tables, with that hideous growling and whining, now barking, never stopping. I'm an evil judge, a tyrant – a wicked and malicious human being.

I need treatment to halt my raging blood; I sweat in the cool evening air like I've a fever. Then perhaps I have: a fever of the blood and brain and ego. I have to plan in detail the repair of the dreadful damage I've caused. I can't bear listening to the howling from the courtyard any longer. It cuts my soul to ribbons and rips my heart in two. She has suffered enough – Nicole must be changed back. But what then? For what I did to her, she will hate me for always with a deep passion.

But a chink of light. Perhaps there is recompense. I need to prove again my yearning for her, show her the guilt riddling through me, show her I can suffer too – no, show her I deserve to suffer.

I will have Lilah transform me as well – become the lowly dog I deserve and cower before Nicole as dog. Be given enlightenment of the torture I'm putting Nicole through.

Yes, return to the courtyard – the everyday one – bury the memory stick for safety, wedge open the doors. Go to Lilah and request I have the power to transform myself when ready; return to Nicole dog. And with a sharp clap of my hands I will suffer excruciating twisting and bending of muscle, the pushing and pulling of internal organs, the tortuous reshaping of bones, exactly like Nicole must have done. I'll stay a dog for as long as it takes to begin the healing process with Nicole, suffering with her and for her. When the pitiful crying and whining has stopped for at least a short while, I will have paid some of my dues. And when there's the beginning of forgiveness I'll have Lilah transform us both back to humans, horrific memories erased; those guests in blissful states awakened; oak trees made as they were and swans returned to proper sizes. Even the pompous receptionist restored, leaving her android persona behind. Did that stranger deserve so much punishment for being party to the liaisons of Nicole and Maurice? And Maurice, does he really deserve such excruciating pain? Let Maurice cease the jogging, his ankle healing instantly; yes, stop the broken ankle agony. Stop the robotic horror. Stop that anguished barking. Be punished. Begin anew.

Now I go.

*****

Email From: Stella Bridgeport 12 June 2013 21:32
To: Audrey Ackerman Dogs at the inn

Dear Audrey, like I said earlier, I don't want you to leave. So the weeks you've already had away and the week in Banchester are irrelevant. I'll say again, you can return whenever you wish. But if you decide to move on I will fully understand. Though even then, you really will be welcome back any time.

Now I've finished the files, they'd make up a great plot for a film, wouldn't they! The romantic love triangle feature, that mostly worked. And the wonder stuff, genies, spectres and ghost dogs, was all quite well written I thought, even if so very out there. To be fair, yes, the puzzle pieces did lock together in the end. All of the other questions answered, definitely. I can even understand your distress seeing Gideon as a dog, staring at you with black pebble eyes, glowing orange spots in the middles. Exactly like the genie's eyes. That does sound freaky.

Goodbye, Audrey, and take great care of yourself. Love to you. If I don't see you before, I hope you have a terrific time in Banchester :) And again I'll say, no rush for decisions. Either way, please keep in touch. Best regards, Stella

•

Email From: Audrey Ackerman   13 June 2013 15:41
To: Stella Bridgeport   Re: Dogs at the inn

Goodbye Stella, thanks again for your kind words. And as you wrote, whatever I decide, I will keep in touch. I hope your day continues well. When I've returned from the Banchester trip, I will be making a truly final decision, that's a promise. Kind regards, Audrey

P.S. Eyes are meant to show aspects of spirit – meant to be windows to the soul, aren't they? When Gideon as a dog looked up at me by the open door of the bedroom, his eyes showed bottomless wells of despair; frightened, almost tortured as though he was about to be judged – yet they weren't the same as Lilah's, black and orange; not even an altered natural brown dog's eyes. No, neither of these. This was a dog possessing a pair of wide open, pleading, human eyes.

HENRIETTA

Slow boil, it's called. Victoria, the elegant and refined older lady who has never shown an ounce of anger, finally reveals her true feelings while nibbling on a cottage cheese and cucumber sandwich.

The sun hides behind a cotton-spun cloud; shadows fade; the sun's reflections in the teacups' contents vanish. Victoria's husband, Bertrand, leans back in his metal chair on the garden patio. He casts an eye over his vegetable patch. And on further, over to a side of the shed lined with pots of shrubs.

'Time,' he says, grinning like a fool. Victoria's cheeks are reddening as she gulps a morsel of sandwich, and locks her sight onto her husband on the opposite side of the wrought iron table. She says nothing in return. Bertrand adds, 'What time, you're meant to say; come on, ol' gal, play the game.'

Tears are misting Victoria's eyes now. She throws the sandwich onto a patterned plate on the table.

'What time is it, Bertrand? I'll tell you what time,' she replies, her high voice loud and strained, 'time for you to choose.'

'Now then, steady on, don't know what you're saying.'

'I'm saying,' Victoria continues, choking back the tears,

'It's either me or Henrietta.'

The sun appears again from behind its cloud. Bertrand has to shield his animated eyes, looking his quivering wife up and down as if studying a museum artefact.

'You're being silly,' Bertrand says. How many times do I visit her? Four times a day, that's all. Feed her sometimes, if she's having trouble. Where's the harm in that? I've even started singing her songs now and then.'

Victoria stands abruptly, wagging a finger.

'You see? You're going round the bend and taking me with you. I've had enough, Bertrand. Choose – now.'

'Easy one, ol' gal. Both. You, with your beautiful summer dress on and wonderful sunhat, getting uppity over nothing; and Henrietta, nicely safe in the shed.'

'In that case, I'm leaving.'

'Don't be silly. Sit down and have another cup of tea.'

'I mean it, Bertrand. I'll be staying at my sister Eileen's house. Leaving tomorrow and won't be back until you see sense.'

Bertrand realizes she is serious. Slightly flustered, he speaks rapidly, occasionally glancing back over to the shed.

'No need to go. I'll see less of her, that's a promise. How's that?'

Still standing, and swaying now, Victoria replies, 'You'll not see her at all. What am I saying: see how you've twisted my mind? You've even got me saying "her". It, Bertrand, a revolting IT!' She slaps a refined palm onto the table and the crockery rattles, before sitting again, tears now readily springing from her distraught eyes.

'Now look here, ol' gal, you can't make me choose.

Henrietta needs me.'

'Needs you, Bertrand?' Victoria says, dabbing her cheeks with a handkerchief taken from one of her dress sleeves. 'You're in need of a psychiatrist. And I need you – to pull yourself together, to leave this madness behind.'

Bertrand takes a deep breath and exhales slowly.

'Not madness – fascination. You can become fascinated too. Come along, ol' gal, let's visit her together. All you have to do is become fond of the incredible creature. Discover what a marvel of nature she is. How could such a small thing come between us? Let me explain again—'

'No more explanations, please…'

'Any spider can produce up to seven different types of silk. The protein fibre spun by the spiders is to make their beautiful, intricate webs. These are their nets to catch other insects, or as cocoons to protect their offspring. They can produce up to five hundred in one season. The web threads are, weight for weight, stronger than steel…'

Victoria interrupts: 'This has become intolerable beyond comprehension, Bertrand.'

She stands hurriedly again, walks across the sun-baked patio and through the open French windows, shutting them behind her.

As if nothing untoward had happened, Bertrand shrugs his shoulders, his silly grin returning. He sips his tea, also stands, and with determination makes his way along the path by the lawn to his shed which is tucked into the garden's end next to the greenhouse.

The shed door creaks when opening, as it always does. Bertrand enters with ceremonial deference, walks past the lawnmower and bags of fertilizer and compost, to the dusty left-hand corner.

'Still happy, my Henrietta?' he says quietly, putting his grey-haired head close to the orb-weaver spider's web. 'I have more flies for you when you're ready.'

As if the brown arachnid understands, it scampers over to the centre of the cobweb from its edge. Its body is the size of an English penny. It has black and white markings.

Bertrand mumbles and exhorts, speaks loudly then softly again, explaining carefully the volatile situation arisen.

Late afternoon, Victoria is quiet, and more so in the early evening – refusing to speak with her husband, other than to say, 'If you haven't changed your mind by tomorrow, I'm moving out. I'll be sleeping in the spare room tonight.'

Bertrand knows she won't be leaving; knows she won't be able to leave.

He spends a restful night alone and, at the insistent ringing of the bedside clock, leaps out of bed with a youthful energy despite his elderly years. He slips downstairs to make breakfast for his wife. She would surely still want her orange juice, and toast and marmalade.

He carefully carries the loaded breakfast tray back up the stairs and gently pushes on the spare bedroom door – already ajar – with his foot.

Bertrand gives his lunatic, lopsided grin upon seeing Victoria laying on top of the bed eiderdown.

She is wrapped tightly in the spun threads from countless spiders. Only her nose is exposed for breathing, and mouth uncovered in a wide open, soundless scream, ready to be fed her breakfast.

CLARA SEAWARD'S PAINTINGS

This is how Clara Seaward remembered her birth: the womb no more than a prison, amniotic fluid as her irritating suspension. Drumbeat of the heart and muffled voices, underlining connections between sounds and the growth of painfulness. She believed her mother had no spiritual blossoming at the moment of delivery, only hatred for the evacuated child. For Clara, the pain of the sores on her skin first registered, as she wailed with a fierce intenseness never heard before.

Nurtured with pain, growing worse as she grew. The prospect of a life ahead filled with pain, woven throughout her spirit, mind and body. Now with sores on her legs and arms, nerve-endings jangling and scraping. Sores about her neck, in her armpits, and over the backs of her hands. More on her heels, making her walk in an unnatural way on the soles of her feet like an ungainly ballet dancer. All inflamed, sensitive and stinging; a constant agony.

When she became a teenager, she took up oil painting, the only positive trait inspired by her father. And upon her sixteenth birthday, she hid herself away in her father's converted windmill studio on the lake island, banishing her parents from visiting. But still her mother visited most days, rowed over the lake by the gardener, to leave food and other provisions outside the door.

Six months had past slowly for Clara, living alone in the windmill studio, her pain still constant. As was her desire to paint her pain and those she believed to be the instigators of it. And within that time, she had always refused every concoction, herbal or pharmaceutical remedy to try to alleviate her symptoms.

For a short while, stillness in the room. A dominant silence in the windmill studio, no clock marking seconds. Either side of the south window stood tall pillars, graceful sentries to the view. A morning without sun, sky smothered by drapes of stagnant clouds. The quiet air broken by howling from the country house, the estate on the mainland hemmed by trees, unseen as though erased by the mist. No wind or slapping waves of the misted lake against the island rocks today.

As Clara sat by the window, her focus was on a newly-spun cobweb over one of the panes. Her hand deftly manipulated an invisible paintbrush. She moved her fingers close to the web, her imagination filling in the shapes that the threads made with solid blocks of vibrant colour.

Clara's heart beat fast: she turned quickly, the speed defying her symptoms, to gaze over at the canvas on the easel. It seemed to look back with an abstract aloofness.

She pushed her young but thin frame to a standing position. Then she walked slowly and with difficulty over to the bentwood chair with its supply of velvet cushions, and sat in front of her easel.

The trembling of Clara’s hand towards a sable brush,

laboured breath and watering eyes, making her artist's studio – a cast of beams spanning the high ceiling – as seen through a filter. Clara inspected the paintbrush taken from a pine table, scrutinizing it as if seeing it for the first time.

The primed pink canvas tempered the textured whiteness, for she had long ago found white to shout, to demand too much attention, to taunt her inspiration.

Without the beats to time – within that stillness and silence – she had learned an act of patience, firm and consistent, requiring the mind to venture into safe territory to wait for the inspired image.

Perhaps extreme emotion creates a frequency, a resonance outside of normal everyday experience. Her mind was squeaking chalk on a blackboard, a single conscious desire to find the wickedness in her parents, any goodness shown by them believing to be a facade, a mere pretence.

Clara knew she was ready, the familiar sense of urgency beneath her ribs. She would prepare something special for her mother's visit today: create an identical picture to the one she had painted six months before. Though this time, she would add to her mother's punishment of talking lies, with an additional aspect – that being one to imply her mother's constant, unwanted intrusion.

She squeezed warm grey onto a pallet before plunging the brush into it, then with bold flourishes on the canvas, began the underpainting. Her vision was blinkered; only the paint drying was important. She continued the underpainting using ochres and pastels, mustards and light blues. Then building the paint, area by area, layer by layer, detail upon detail.

She painted fast and within a heart-felt passion when within her fugue – until three hours later, there finished on the canvas, with a background of a room in the country house, was a perfectly rendered portrait. Delicate and detailed, showing a beautiful older woman seated upon a chair, painted without a mouth. And between the fulsome, sparkling eyes of the portrait, Clara had added, in perfect clarity, a third eye.

Clara sat at the easel for a full hour, still, and waiting.

A timid knocking on the windmill artist's studio door.

Clara put down her paintbrush and turning to the door, called out, 'Come in today, I want to see.'

The door opened and her mother, Sara-Lyn, entered Clara's studio, almost furtively. Her head was lowered, and covered with a shawl. Her face covered as well, with just her two eyes showing. She clutched a wicker basket to her side, the contents wrapped with a tea towel. She walked to a table which stood next to the window, unpacked the basket, and extracted a plate of hot food, some bread and cheese, and a yoghurt. The last items she took out were a notepad and a pencil.

Clara walked back over to the south window, on the balls of feet, to inspect her mother's face hidden behind the shawl. 'Take it off, mother.'

Sara-Lyn ignored her daughter's order and opened the notepad, showing Clara the first page, words written upon it. At first, Clara refused to look until, with impatience, she glanced at it and read, "Please eat properly today."

'I eat enough,' Clara said.

Clara read from the second page, "Can we talk? How

could you punish me like this? I have difficulty breathing through my nose – I won't be able to eat. Would you want me to feed myself with a tube; do you want me to die?"

'You won't die, mother,' Clara replied, 'only your grating, annoying rasp of voice will continue to be silenced. And we both know the reason for that, don't we.'

She turned the page of the notebook and read, "When will you help us?"

Clara's mother undid the shawl and took it away from her face. Her third eye, placed neatly in the middle of her forehead, above her normal left and right, blinked independently and involuntarily. She had no mouth. She went to the large settee in a darkened corner and sat, leaning forward, her refined head put to the side in anticipation of the answer.

Clara touched between the cracked sores on her cheek. She narrowed her haunted eyes with an extraordinary expression marring her features, threatening anger and fear. Her eyes refocused: the reflection in the glass of the window smoothed the dappling of burst veins and erased the scars and scabs on her chin, the warm brunette of this young woman's hair seeming purple; her wicked smile, warm.

More howls of screeching anguish were carrying over on a gusting breeze from somewhere in the country house. Clara's mother wrote in the notepad and showed it to Clara.

"Do you hear your father; hear his pain?"

'Could I have possibly done more?' Clara said in reply. 'Given him three eyes as well, or a head like a stag beetle? Or eight legs even, skittering in search for his slippers?' She sniggered and snuffled, despite the pain from the sores on her neck.

"I have something important to tell. Please – release my mouth," Sara-Lyn wrote in the notepad and showed it to her daughter.

Clara looked with suspicion at her mother's three weeping eyes. Then, shrugging, she walked under the spotlights as if on stage, towards the canvas on its easel. The table beside it was littered with paint tubes, a pallet, linseed oil and mottled rags.

She sat on her chair and began to paint a mouth onto her mother's portrait.

After ten minutes, the image was corrected, and Clara looked over to see her mother with her mouth again.

Sara-Lyn bowed her head.

'You think that this can go on forever, don't you? Haven't you realised that you are close to the end?' Sara-Lyn looked up suddenly, all three eyes glaring with determination and condemnation.

'Is that all you wanted to say? Some sort of threat? Careful, or I'll paint over your vicious mouth again.'

I mean,' Clara's mother continued, 'You are close to finally accepting the truth. I know you are a good heart, that deep down you are hurting yourself even more than you are hurting your father and I. Your cruelness to yourself and us are the same thing: all part of your self-harm. You must understand, Clara. How much longer can this go on, all of us trapped in a damnation, your damnation?'

Tears sprang from her eyes, including the extra organ of sight, for it was symmetrical, a tear-duct either side of it.

The wind quietened; the baboon-like howling from the

house on the mainland ceased.

A pause, Clara curling her top lip until she replied in a quiet, almost whispered voice, despite fury building again from within.

'Why do you always speak such dull, silly nonsense?' She picked up a paintbrush and turning it the other way around, she clutched it by the brush end, brown umber smearing her palm. Then she strode across to Sara-Lynn, her clenched fist with knuckles white, threatening the brush as if it were a sharp knife, jabbing it towards her third eye. 'You don't want your third eye?' she cried out, 'then I'll poke it out for you; better still, scoop it out with a palette knife.'

'No, not like that!' Sara-Lynn cried out and ran from Clara towards the cottage door.

Then tears sprang from Clara's eyes, finding a way down her face, travelling between the intricate pattern of sores as if water finding a course over cracked mud. 'Wait, mother, I can't bear the pain any more.'

Her mother turned to say, 'Your tears tell me you can believe! I would cuddle you – comfort you if I could. Help your father, help yourself, help me! Let me explain again now you have given back my mouth to speak. This time you must listen – and believe that what I say is the truth.

'You have not been well, Clara. Your eating disorder, your delusions and self-harming. Shutting yourself away here, in your father's studio for all these months. But what fabulous talent you have, to paint with such nuance, vibrancy, detail and passion. Your father told me – when he could speak words – you surpass him in talent.'

'Say that again? You never told me this before,' Clara

replied, her damaged forehead ruffling.

'I did tell you, but you weren't listening. Yes, it's true, you have immense artistic talent. And the magic of bringing into being anything you paint is unique to the world.' Clara could see a fierce passion burning in her mother's three eyes. 'You must accept that to repair what has been done is forgiveness of yourself. You know you have the solution.

'Your series of self portraits from birth to now, showing sores and blisters ruining your skin. I'll explain again and you must believe me this time. You weren't born with them. When you were three, you ran into me while I carried a pan of boiling water. You were scalded badly, this is true; you had severe burns but they healed. But not your mind, Clara. You have tortured yourself through false memories that you were born with sores, that you've had them all your life. But that's not true. You've tortured yourself for torturing your father and I.'

'Do I trust you? Why should you help me after what I have done?'

Clara's mother shut all three eyes and spoke quietly, 'Because I love you, my dear daughter.' Clara was on the balls of her feet again, her arms held away from her, and she went to Sara-Lyn. Despite stinging pain she would have to endure, she threw her arms about her mother.

'Repair is simple,' Sara-Lyn continued. 'You have shielded the truth from yourself for too long. You must paint again like the wind, rain and sun talk to me: calming, graceful, powerful. You only need the will, the grace and optimism for your future. And your family's future. Paint another portrait of your father, erase the head of an ape you have given him, give back his original handsome features; paint out my third eye, then paint a final self-portrait. Paint yourself without burns, without sores, and so without pain.'

RETURN TO THE SEA

As Lucas clambered over slate-blue rocks on the even expanse of sand, his world changed. The beach, a pastel orange stripe, to him had quickly become luminous, the cries from the black-headed gulls by the cliff top heard as scornful laughter.

Heat drained the air. His tongue curled in a parched mouth. The empty wine bottle he held slipped from his fingers and clattered across a boulder, catching on mollusc shells as it went. He tottered backwards, fell onto a slab of rock, seeing the sky turning to chalk, the sea to mercury. Even the gusting wind had changed in quality for him. Its sound was now babbling voices, and the waves hissed as if made from rustling leaves.

An illogical idea was born: he must instruct the seascape, reshape it back into normality, direct it as easily as he did his actors and actresses on the London stages.

The gulls were swooping from their crags, screeches transforming into speech as the gusts became a breeze. And as that breeze vanished to leave unmoving air, he understood the utterance, '—not waiting any longer.'

Lucas stood in a clumsy fashion, scanning the wall of rock and sandstone, attempting to identify the source of the voice.

Over to his left, the coastline was a hunched shoulder. This high cliff dipped generously directly above him before rising again to another dramatic shoulder of granite the other side. He looked upwards. At the summit, in that cliff valley, stood a young woman wearing a summer dress and a sunhat. Even from thirty feet away, Lucas could see his wife Evelyn with her attractive face marred with annoyance. A short distance from her, the shuttered upper windows of a house could be spied between gaps in the foliage of oak trees.

A sense of place and reason again: of course, he realized, he had returned to the summer cottage, was on the beach in the cove below, hunting for pebbles and shells for his wife. He shouted up to her as best he could, a dire exhaustion sapping his energy.

'Don't move an inch, Evelyn. Be with you in two ticks.'

He trod up the sandy slope, the path littered with stones, earth piles, and fallen tree trunks, their roots still compacted with clay. His heart beat dangerously fast. He stopped several times to allow the pounding within his chest to lessen. Now even heavy rocks either side of the path, as well as the clinging shrubs, appeared bleached; and to his ears they sang with a whine like any bowed violin string.

A coil of barbed wire lay beside the path with wire cutters next to it. Lucas stopped there, creasing his brow as if not understanding. Then, through a haze, he remembered snipping the wire a while back and kicking it out of the way.

His attention was broken by the same woman's shrill voice cutting the sultry air, 'What did you call me?'

Lucas reached her at the top, with a splendid countryside behind, bright in the sun. For him, the fields and hedgerows in the valley had become a strange swirl of pastel colours, and his wife unusually animated with annoyance, anger even. The dizziness overtook again and he swayed while passing a hand across his forehead. Sweat trickled from his sodden shirt collar down his spine. Although feeling unwell, he attempted to lighten the situation.

'Chill out, Evelyn, this isn't like you. I'll open another red; or even get water—' he licked his dry lips, 'yes, water; I could drink a horse trough.'

'Of course you could, silly man. Look at you, with your lobster face. You're dehydrated, more than likely got sunstroke. Your brain's addled even more than usual. There's no water, it's been cut off, remember? Like the electricity. Why you brought me to this derelict place I can't imagine. And you called me Evelyn again.' Samantha had hold of wedge shoes and she let them go for them to fall onto the grass. While she wiggled one of her feet into a shoe, with a hand flat on top of her sunhat, she said, 'Sun drunk or not, I'm fed up with you keep calling me that.' She inclined her head, expecting an answer, just as Evelyn might have done.

If it wasn't for the makeup and different hairstyle, she could pass for Evelyn on occasions. Still, in the six months that Lucas had known Samantha, he found her to be a contradictory woman every time they were together, as if she used her skills as an actress to act out each day differently.

She came into focus. He saw no patterned summer dress upon her but a low-cut blouse and a knee-length, beige skirt.

'I don't know what's happening,' Lucas muttered. 'You're right, the sun's got to me.'

'And the drink.'

His breathing became rapid.

'Not that much. You had more.'

'Other way around,' Samantha replied. 'You took the second bottle. I only drank a glassful. Still, I'm not going to argue. I've had enough of waiting around.'

'Not been that long. Hang on—' He tried to slow his breathing by clutching his chest.

'Stop showing off, Lucas.' A pause, then, 'You were gone ages. It can't take that long to cut a few bits of barbed wire.'

Lucas saw, in his mind's eye, snapshots of the last half an hour: arriving at the cottage for the first time in two years; outrage at the signs on the doors. The upset when reading official letters insisting he could no longer live there. Shock at how little of the garden was intact. Cursing and swigging from the wine bottle as he made his way down to the beach to view the remains of the pergola lodged between rocks, the ornate sundial and birdbath half-buried in the sand, the garden bench upended as though it had been casually thrown away. Winter storms had created mighty waves, battered the cliff face, eroded dry soil and caused landslides, clawed the apple and cherry trees to fall away first, followed by the summerhouse and the rest.

Samantha added, 'There's no wine left and anyway, who wants to be in your excuse of a house.'

Lucas looked along the short avenue of oak trees to the red-bricked cottage that seemed to slump all at once as if the sun had become a pressure on its mossed roof.

He walked slowly over to one of the trees and into its shadow. 'How was I to know this happened? Why the council couldn't trace me I really don't know. It wasn't like this when

I was here with Evelyn.'

'That's done it. Give me your car keys, I want them, now,' Samantha ordered.

Lucas shook his muddled head. All at once he saw a glowing figure with an arm outstretched, its palm exposed, fused fingers jabbing his stomach.

'Car keys? What for?'

'I've already said. You can pick up the car from outside your flat. And don't expect me to be there either; I'm moving back with Martin. That's what I want.'

'You dumped Martin a year ago. Why would you want to go back to him?' Samantha looked away and blew air though her nose. Lucas was used to her random irritability but with the way he was feeling with the effects of alcohol and the sun, he had no patience with tantrums and idle threats today. 'Then don't expect to be in the cast anymore,' he added.

His words immediately rearranged her scowling face. Her tone became softer as she stroked his unruly hair.

'Don't be like that, Lucas. You'd be crazy to push me out. Who else can deliver those intricate lines like I do. Come on, let me borrow your car. How am I meant to walk in these shoes? You won't mind catching a train from the town. Please?' Her face appeared lit with more than sunshine.

He felt bilious, screwing his eyelids over his dried and irritated eyes.

'Evelyn; she's not here,' he said.

Samantha studied him with vague concern. 'That's a start, I suppose.'

Then, with a starling flapping away from a pollarded beech tree, he turned away from her and staggered towards the cottage gate.

'Hey, what about the keys,' she called out and hurried after him.

They went through the bentwood arch and over the patio and reached the front entrance, either side shrouded by climbing roses. Lucas ripped the sign from the open door and read again, "Danger, Keep Out. Condemned as Dangerous and Unsafe." Samantha stayed under the porch, while he entered the cottage.

It was cooler inside, a comfortable room with an open fireplace and heavy lintel, overstuffed armchairs and bookshelves, an antique typewriter crouching in a corner. A door to the kitchen stood next to the staircase. There were photographs of ships on the walls between stuffed fish mounted in wooden boxes. Beams spanned overhead. Pine tables stood at the sides, covered with magazines, pebbles and seashells, paintbrushes and other artist's paraphernalia.

Beachcombing had become obsessive for Lucas whenever he and Evelyn had stayed at their sea view cottage. Happy to wander over the beach, much had caught his eye or imagination with the hope it would hold some artistic merit for Evelyn's creative needs. Whether a trilobite chipped out from the base of the cliff, a stone with interesting striations or an unusual seashell, it would have been inspected before washing in a rock pool, then placed in a canvas satchel.

Evelyn had always rummaged through the new collection with enthusiasm, sometimes her hands trembling with excitement to discover what new fascinations the sea had given her as gifts. And those found objects, when placed about calligraphed phrases within frames made of driftwood, became sought-after works of art. They would be displayed in the gallery hidden in a lane behind the palm-fronted town promenade.

One of Evelyn's works hung beside the kitchen door. Lucas was compelled to follow the flowing lines of type painted in watercolour, reading, "The sea, like time, flows endlessly and will be for evermore."

He felt lost, as if in a dream. Still hallucinating through dehydration and heatstroke, an overpowering sensation made him giddier. Evelyn could be conjured to being; she could be made to return. The conviction gripped him. It was as if the click of two fingers would be enough for the garden to be restored, even the rose bushes pruned, with Evelyn standing over one of the tables, intent within her creative energies.

Samantha finally came into the cottage and his dream state was broken. She was searching the room for the car keys. Lucas gave a resigned shrug and pointed to them laying on a shelf. As she went to pick them up, he could do no more than open and close his mouth.

She snatched up the keys and whispered, 'Cry, silly man.' Brushing past him now, she said, 'Catch you later. And find some water before you drop. See, I'm not all bad.'

She went out in a hurry.

Without warning, jolts pulsed through Lucas as painful as any electrical shock – a truth not accepted for two years, finally exposed: Evelyn would never be returning. Nor would the cottage, once the waves had eaten more of the earth away and it was sent crashing into the sea below.

He turned to the window and, as though waiting for an answer, fixed his sight onto tiny boats lonely in the distance, the sea glinting there as if alive with sparks.

A conclusion snapped into mind, clear-cut and impossible to refute. If Evelyn would never come back to him, he would return to her. But as crystalline as this thought was, still it belonged to a man not in full control of his senses. It was a dizzy resolve, made with the sensation of spinning in a circle, revolving on a nauseous merry-go-round.

He lurched towards the doorway. Despite his dire sickness from the sun's rays, he left the cottage and paced across the garden – what remained of the garden – towards the cliff edge.

Swaying at the brink now and looking down to debris, and soil which once had been organized and tended, there below in untidy heaps between rocks and tide pools, and swathes of quicksand decorated with streaks of seaweed.

The hushed melody from the sea was no match for the pumping in his ears. Back he went to the gate, along the line of trees, then over to the beginning of the slope. Samantha was sitting in the driver's seat of his car but at the sight of him she turned on the ignition, crunched the gears into reverse, and swung the car backwards in a semi-circle.

Lucas began the walk back down the slope. His arms were held out as though he might be sleepwalking.

When he reached the hot sand he stood trance-like for a minute before treading over to the sea's ragged edge. The surf lapped at his shoes. Instantly, a vision, a projection of a vivid memory, overlaid perfectly before him — the open oak casket decorated with flowers and seashells, lit candles flickering inside, giving a yellow cast to the bundles of poems and the container of ashes, the whole arrangement gently bobbing on the dark water stained with moonlight.

Quickly, harsh sun returned. Stumbling onward, splashing through the breaking waves, wading further until the sea was up to his waist.

Overwhelmed all at once, low sobs emanating from him in jerking, regular pulses as if he was expressing with some ancient native tongue, tears making tracks down his pained face.

He bellowed Evelyn's name, a drawn-out roar filled with anguish, and the waves roared back the same. The cliff became massive arms, drawing together with a clamour to smother him, his world now no more than a velvet shroud. He collapsed to his knees onto shingle with only his head visible above the seawater until even that vanished.

'Silly man,' Samantha was repeating while she hauled him up, her arms under his armpits. While she was dragging him to the shallows he awoke, coughing and spluttering. He stood in panic but seemed willing to be led. Samantha held his hand and pulled him towards the beach. And once there, she held onto his swaying form to steady him, then snatched a bottle of water from the sand. 'Drink this. It was in the boot of your car.'

Lucas twisted the cap off and drank greedily until half of the liquid was gone. While wiping his mouth and panting, he handed the bottle to Samantha and she drank from it too.

They sat in their soaked clothes at the water's edge, watching those constant waves, until she said quietly, 'You wanted to be with her, didn't you?' He nodded, his head hanging low with dark hair plastered flat, and skin glistening with water droplets. 'You will, one day.' Lucas looked up to inspect her olive-green eyes. They held an indefinable depth within, a mysterious strength. 'But until then you won't call me Evelyn.'

He seemed to brighten before saying, 'And you won't call me silly man anymore.'

'Now where's the fun in that?' Samantha replied. Lucas caught the subtlest of smiles from her, those beautiful eyes shining with a kind of love. She continued, 'I think the tide's going out. Let's go home. Together. That's what I really want.'

And as they stood, wind blew from across the sea again, its gusts sounding as if spoken words. Lucas inclined an ear and heard a compelling, faraway voice say, 'Come to me.'

A CROUCHING MAN

How much longer should I crouch, here by my gate? Is it my gate anymore? Starting to rain but still can't move to a standing position despite the incredible aching in my limbs. I'm startled, shocked into submission. When I do dare venture inside the house I'll no doubt walk while crouching, like some strange two legged animal shuffling along.

I must catalogue the events of this morning in my mind. Try to find some sense as to how this all could have happened – how I could have let it happen.

The start of today was happy and bright; making me happy and bright enough to want to paint our front gate. The tin of stove enamel black had been sitting on the garage shelf for too long – time to use it, I thought.

The gate to our two up, two down Victorian terraced house is identical to the one directly opposite, as is the house. Like a mirror image, like all the houses in the terrace each side of the road.

Get yourself out there, get the gate finished, Fiona had said.

Why she had become so short-tempered over the last few weeks I didn't know.

I placed a dust sheet under the gate to prevent any paint spillage on the path or pavement. And after shaking the tin, prised off the paint lid with the end of a screwdriver. Dipped the brush into the black, and began my task of painting the front gate, from the top.

Standing and painting in the morning sunshine, I did begin to enjoy the process, almost cathartic in its own way – even whistled while I worked.

It was then I noticed him, the new neighbour who had moved into the identical-looking house directly opposite. He was crouching, and painting his gate from the bottom upwards with black paint. I remember waving over in a friendly way, and him staring, almost glaring back. I did feel confused and slightly indignant at his reaction to my friendliness. Sure, we hadn't been formally introduced, although Fiona had told me she had said hello and welcomed him into the street when he moved into number 77 a month ago.

I continued painting the top rungs of my gate but every time I glanced up, there was that neighbour glaring back at me in a distinctly antagonistic manner. I lowered my head and hurried into the house, so disturbing did I find it.

'He might or might not be friendly, how am I expected to know,' Fiona had said. 'Get back to it and finish the job.'

I felt slightly foolish at becoming so agitated that I immediately went back out to the front garden to carry on.

I tried my best to ignore the fellow across the road, though I became almost certain of two things: the further down I painted my wrought iron gate, the further up he painted his wrought iron gate. And from the periphery of my vision I saw he was somehow painting without looking at what he was doing, constantly staring at me.

After half of an hour, I had painted half of the gate and was, at that point, bending at the waist. It was then I dared to look directly back over at the man at 77. He had reached the same point on his gate and he also stood bending. A passing pedestrian might have thought we were bowing deeply to each other. Still his sight was fixed upon me.

I studied him the more: he was even wearing the same coloured overalls I'm wearing, and as far as I could make out, similar brown, work shoes.

I stood upright and as I did, so did he. I placed the paintbrush to rest on the tin lid – opposite, a moment later, the same. And wiping paint from one of my hands onto a trouser leg of my overalls I noticed he was doing the same again.

How could a mirror life exist in reality without any mirrors? I was baffled and hurried back inside to clear my head before carrying on. I needed a drink to calm my agitation.

After calling Fiona and getting no reply, I made myself a cup of coffee and sat by the net curtains in the front room, wondering if I should look to the copycat opposite. Finally I did peak out from behind the curtains. He had gone.

Or at least I thought he had, until I saw him, that weird neighbour across the road, looking from behind his curtains over to me, still the scowl engrained upon his features.

This was becoming annoying, so much that I considered marching over there, rapping on his door to ask for an explanation.

But first, I decided I must finish my set task of painting the gate. So, after I had drunk half of the coffee, once more I walked out to the front garden to continue painting.

Did I expect the neighbour to be doing the same, walking down towards his front gate? I can't remember, but do remember a slight repugnance at this continuing copycat behaviour, as he did that very thing, both of us reaching our respective gates at the same time.

I made the decision to ignore him for the while, so as to concentrate on painting the rest of my front garden gate, from the middle to the bottom of it.

When painting the last bars, I crouched, as I still am now. Unable to move, mesmerized by what I saw at number 77.

The neighbour opposite had stood upright, having finished painting his gate; and instead of a grimace, his eyes fixed upon mine once more and he gave a devilish grin. At that moment, his front door opened and a young woman trotted down the path, also grinning in an exaggerated, crazy way. It was Fiona.

THE CONVERSION OF RUSCOE ROBINSON

A forest can be a fragrant sanctuary of relaxation, a retreat for contemplation amidst its tranquillity — or else a dangerous foe, a hate-filled place to avoid before it engulfs you…

Sebastian and his friend from the city mounted their bikes when they had reached the lane. Assuming Ruscoe was following, Sebastian set off with enthusiasm through the archway of mossy boughs. He was glad of cooler air over his hot limbs.

He passed the churchyard with headstones crumbling and copper trunks of beech in groves. A gentle incline led to open fields. Pasture and lush slopes beyond the river were saturated with summer. The farmer had reached the picnic area at the margin of the forest before looking back to see Ruscoe several minutes away. Sebastian enjoyed the sun and watched grazing sheep for a while with a professional interest.

He had not seen his university companion of old for a year. Yet since arriving that morning, Ruscoe had acted as a stranger; or worse, as if he bore a grudge. Though piqued by this unusual behaviour and puzzled by the change in his comrade, Sebastian had refused to react. He would not pry but wait to be confided in, being mild-mannered and fond of his friend. 'The chap's eccentric, that's all; too many brain cells,' Sebastian had concluded.

From a distance, Ruscoe Robinson was perceived as remembered: dignified albeit lanky as he marched with a purposeful gait, a scribble of hair, and intelligent, probing eyes. But as the skinny man neared, Sebastian saw again crucial changes twelve months had made. Ruscoe stooped with shoulders hunched (although pushing a bicycle in the oppressive heat did not help his posture); and his unruly hair had turned grey and patchy. Those eyes – which once seemed to examine the soul – appeared dull and lifeless.

He arrived gasping and shakily patted his perspiring forehead. Then he removed his backpack to take from it a carton of drink and sunglasses.

Sebastian studied his distressed friend with concern — seeing wasted muscles through Ruscoe's tight clothing, his drawn face turned pink and puffy, with eyebrows frowning and covered then by the dark lenses.

'Chain came off, ' Ruscoe stated before holding out the oily palm of a hand as if in proof. He gulped draughts of liquid from the carton.

Intense work has exhausted him, made him ill even, Sebastian guessed.

'Are you sure you're alright? We can go back to the farmhouse if you prefer.'

Ruscoe seemed to brighten.

'No problem, I've come this far —'

Rather than continue along the lane, they decided to ride at a gentle pace through the forest. Despite the atmosphere there being a refreshing tranquilliser, this holiday was no more than a nasty medicine to Ruscoe: a necessary though unenjoyable experience.

The afternoon grew older. The pair had stopped by a large elm tree.

'Good exercise!' Sebastian uttered earnestly. 'Well my friend, worn out yet?'

Ruscoe answered with an unexpected breathy monotone, as though three words were an effort to produce.

'I . . . think . . . so', he managed to say.

Upon meeting the farmer again after wearisome months in the city, Ruscoe had wanted desperately to hug Sebastian and to thank him for his hospitality. But he had been unable to, for he was trapped in a cage behind those tortured eyes, with his body made of unfeeling sponge. He had taken more prescribed tablets a few hours ago. Certainly he had taken too many — but rather that than not enough, he believed. At least he was not quaking. He looked up to see Sebastian eyeing him with concern.

'Working too many hours, bit out of sorts,' Ruscoe mumbled, in an attempt to explain his attitude. He fell silent and stared to his watch.

Stretching his arms as if in a relaxed state of mind, Sebastian was nonetheless becoming annoyed at what he viewed as self-pity.

'Listen here, Russ, snap out of it. Forget your concrete and glass; relax and taste a bit of real living. There's more to life than a mainframe and a bunch of algorithms. Too many computer screens and cigarettes, that's been your trouble. Let go from that, for a week at least.'

All Ruscoe could do was nod though pleased with his friend's apparent concern.

Sebastian was eager for more brisk exercise. He possessed an athletic build and metabolism, and these demanded exertion. He felt he must shake Ruscoe from his depression.

'I'm game for more action. Reckon you could keep up?' he challenged with a grin.

Before a reply could be mustered, the forest had swallowed him.

Ruscoe took a deep breath and rode off in pursuit.

He came to a halt with his chest heaving and brought his watch to eye level. Even this minor invention was superior to anything nature could produce, Ruscoe thought, with its clever interaction of miniature elements, the only decaying piece being the quartz crystal. And this verged on the supernatural – he considered – with its uncanny ability to slice time into fragments. The sweep hand moved second by second and it somehow reassured him.

He was certain Sebastian would be waiting ahead, so he pedalled at a relaxed speed. Around a bend were large plates of earth and chalk, being the exposed undersides of trees, fallen from the autumn storm; and piles of logs with their striated bark peeling in curls. Scarred stumps populated the area like a collection of plinths. A spluttering noise began which Ruscoe believed came from a chainsaw. The track veered left to reveal, through the thin green trunks, a meadow ringed with poplars and bathed in sunlight. He threw down his bike with urgency and after kicking aside nettles and ferns, wove through the wood to the edge. A swathe of brambles divided him from the expanse of grass. What he had thought to be a chainsaw was the sonorous buzz of model aeroplanes weaving and diving about the turquoise sky as expertly as swallows. The few clouds were mere dry brush strokes. A spaniel scampered amongst the heather. Ruscoe had an impulse to know the time again: it was six-thirty. The sun glinted in the glass. Then a flash of red and white from the other side caught his eye: Sebastian stood on a terrace over by the river. He was waving with one hand and raising a glass of beer with the other, as if giving a toast. The Waterside Inn – bright in the sunshine – bisected the terrace with a slab of shadow. Opposite, shielded by overgrown umbrellas, people in bright clothes sat luxuriating in the warmth of the afternoon.

The scene became too real: super-real, like a mirage or a waking dream. Ruscoe hurried back amongst the shady trees and set off on his bike in haste. He considered Sebastian must have followed the track rather than chance scratched legs from the brambles.

He was thirsty, his buttocks sore from the saddle, and all muscles depleted of energy. If only he had more tablets; a nagging sense of unfounded panic was taking hold. He wished for the protective armour of the city, away from this random world of browns and greens.

Surely these battalions of trees should have made way for the meadow? At least five minutes had passed, yet the forest was becoming denser, as if the trunks were shuffling together to form compact ranks. Even birds had been seemingly excluded and the absence of their song was unnerving. The lofty tops of the trees reached high enough to catch a breeze and their leaves hissed. Without warning, a wood-pigeon screeched and flapped untidily across Ruscoe's path. He was startled and almost lost control of his bike as it wobbled dangerously. With a curse, he pedalled with more determination. He threw glances to the left and right, an uneasy sensation of being observed taking hold. He would surely be in the open soon.

Though how much further could it be?

Once more he looked to his timepiece and stared at it with indignation. The hands still showed six-thirty: his new watch had stopped.

On he went, becoming more tired and confused, for his logic was of no use here. He had endeavoured to make educated guesses when coming across forks in the footpath but there was no way of knowing if these decisions were correct.

If only he had brought a compass. The tracks were becoming less defined, less trodden; more branches curled across his way like dead snakes, and flints and jagged stones threatened to puncture his tyres. His skin itched and he felt dazed, sure signs that effects of his medicine were wearing off.

He began to despise the close-knit, dingy location with its quiet anonymity and potential dangers waiting and unseen. There was only confusion and disorientation to be found. This was far removed from the disciplines of science; a stringent, sterile world which he could grasp and comprehend. Worrying and peculiar conjecture came to him then. What if he were to be trapped within this illogical randomness? He would die for sure. But this shouldn't be the place, buried under the vegetable mass — he should be shrouded by concrete, metal and glass, comforted by his beloved computers and books. He did not belong; he was misplaced. Rip open his skull and there might be a neural network of clicking binary switches and his guts full of silicon chips and tripe-coloured circuit boards.

Ruscoe stopped abruptly and shook his head to rid himself of the absurd notions. The situation was becoming ridiculous. He bellowed out the name of his friend but the only reply was from leaves in the breeze. If he listened intently to the susurration, ritualistic syllables and reverential sibilants could be distinguished, as solemn and ancient as the planet itself. It was clear this vast overgrown area knew of his contempt of it, the hushed murmuring being passed along from copse to thicket, from spinney to covert; so that wherever he went, it would know of him and would be expecting him.

All sense of time fled. He had no idea as to how long he had been riding. After trying to solve this frustrating puzzle of escape without any tangible clues; after battling through hedges and banks of lavender; after pushing along winding lanes of sprawling trees, he finally discarded the bike and slumped down onto bracken, utterly fatigued. Straw was caught in his hair and insect bites swelled on his ankles. He drank the last of the liquid from the carton taken from the backpack, and it refreshed his parched mouth.

He must pull himself together. What would a trapper or woodman do in a situation like this? Of course — he would follow the sun. If he were to climb a tree, not only would he note the direction the sun travelled but might – if high enough – espy some landmark which he could aim for.

Ruscoe left the bicycle were it lay and went into the woods to find a suitable specimen worthy of his task.

Perhaps it had not been such a commendable idea after all. He had clambered up onto a bough of a massive oak wreathed in woodbine, but then his stamina had failed him and he could go no further. And viewing upwards into the inner sanctum of the tree with his jaw dropped, he had concluded that even if he possessed the necessary strength, it would be impossible to see above the highest branches. He climbed down and lurched onward, becoming agitated and worried.

Hidden deep within the wildness sat the burnt-out, crumpled shell of a car. It was orange with rust, and ebony with soot and dirt. Devoid of tyres, it balanced on four pedestals of bricks. All windows had been smashed except the windscreen which was intact, though clouded into a crazy jigsaw of glass grains. Its bonnet gaped like some prehistoric beast, with most of the engine long gone from out the grim mouth. The roof was concave indicating that someone had jumped violently upon it. A spindly sapling had found its way up through the floor and out of the back window. The seats were piled to the side and in their place were plastic bags bulging with rubbish.

Ruscoe stared at the wreck. He could have believed that he had been the only one to have trodden over the mulch and moss here. Surely then, if a car had been driven this far, a road was near?

At first, he assumed that the lack of detail and depressing gloom descending was due to tiredness but realised with a jolt that it was getting darker. He hacked at the bushes and nettles with a stick and kicked aside trailing vines as he zigzagged through the thicket, desperate now to see light. The forest was smothering him. He began to pant like a dog as a sickening claustrophobia took hold of his brow. Deeper shadows were forming all over — behind crops of bushes, around knobbled roots writhing from the base of trees and, as if with a purple dye, smearing the definitions of the trunks further away, making them indistinguishable from one another.

If only he had explained all to Sebastian (a man whose understanding and sincerity were unswerving) he might not be here now. But Ruscoe could not bring himself to tell of unbearable pressures accumulating within; of how he needed medication to keep from the cliff-edge of a nervous breakdown; or explain his neglect of wife Sarah who had moved to her mother's home, unable to cope with his dark moods; or how he had become impotent, not only sexually but socially. Being too concerned with the inner state made him ignore all outside of himself.

Ruscoe's mind had been churning and grinding – as unstoppable and powerful as huge cog-wheels – to produce a convoluted introspection. So wrapped up was he with his thoughts, he had barged through the forest without conscious decisions as to his direction.

Coming upon the abandoned car again, the realisation that he had gone in a large circle slapped his face. How could he be so foolish! What was worse, the mass of trees gave no indication as to the direction of where his bike lay.

Ruscoe fell to his knees in a melodramatic fashion and, wringing his hands, he wept uncontrollably. It was an ugly weeping with his face contorted and teeth bared. The tears were for being weary and angry and frustrated at the wasted hours spent. With his city persona calm and logical hiding inside the shaking torso, he felt somehow detached from this alien emotion. The realisation that it was the first time he had cried since childhood washed through him and encouraged the tears. The jerking of his chest was almost painful, but after reaching the climax of his outpouring, he found it a strangely satisfying experience with some of his tension released.

The dusky foliage loomed menacingly above as if preparing to envelop him and the trunks were creeping, it seemed, imperceptibly closer. He took the backpack off and threw it aside, eyeing about him with suspicion. Although his stomach gurgled with hunger then and he was frightened, he let his smarting eyelids fall, and he slept.

That evening he dreamed of Sarah; and of clattering machines; and of death as substance, crouched in brooding places filled with stillness and expectancy; then of nothing. His distress and weakness dragged him down and he plummeted into a well of non-being.

As morning approached, Ruscoe bounced to semi-consciousness now and then, enough to pat the bracken as though plumping his pillow or to sleepily look about in disorientation, not quite sure why the bedroom walls had changed in texture. It had been a hot and sticky night although his rest had been more comfortable than most: those folk kicking their bedclothes from them, annoyed that their open windows did not have any effect on their stuffy and airless rooms.

His eyes sprang open. At first, Ruscoe was bewildered as to his whereabouts but then the events of the day before came to mind in quick sequence. The once threatening boles encircling him were now mere picturesque, leafy trunks, accented with diluted ochre light, the spaces between filled with mist. Birds sang their patterns and the air was fresh, carrying with it aromatic odours.

He stood with difficulty, and stretched wide his arms and legs. They ached and were stiff. He felt surprisingly clear-headed although he shook with coldness from the morning air. Sitting on the wing of the car, he briskly rubbed his thighs and shoulders to muster warmth into them whilst considering his plan of action. If he were to move steadfastly forward in any one direction, he would inevitably come out. This forest could not go on forever. However, before anything else, he must eat and drink.

But where was the backpack? It could not have been thrown far. He searched amongst the dock leaves and grass until he came upon his sunglasses with the scratched lenses pointed blindly to the sky. From this marker, Ruscoe discovered a trail of the contents leading into the woods. His handkerchief draped over a thistle; a split carton lay with an inch of fluid remaining; pens and a ripped notepad, matches and paperbacks all had been scattered at random. And there at the end of this maddening paperchase was his plastic raincoat trailing – like a yellow intestine – from the backpack. Littered about it were scraps of his sandwiches and the silver foil clawed into shreds.

'You swines!' Ruscoe screamed. Some furry wild thing has done this, he concluded. More than likely a fox or badger.

He collected up the belongings and dumped them into the savaged backpack with disgust. How he despised this evil place with all his soul. Disheartened, he sat propped up by a wing of the car. He looked like a doll with arms flaccid beside him, his head lolling and eyes glazed and unseeing. Why not give up the fight and accept the inevitable? An image of his decomposing remains came to him, rotting in this precise position, and it prompted him to move. He must not be beaten — he would find the way out. Clutching the backpack with his bony fingers, he paced through the forest more determined than ever.

The place was alive. As if for the first time, he noticed movement amongst the ferns as a mammal made a hasty departure, a sudden flurry of leaves, or a quick bird darting by. Sunlight, finding gaps in the foliage, licked his face with warm shafts and the cool air invigorated him. Ruscoe checked his watch. Still it showed six-thirty but whatever the time might be, he would have rattled his tablets from the bottle and poured whisky by now. He was pleased with himself for although he felt the need of these, the desire was an easy one to control.

Without presage, a clearing stocked with sunflowers presented itself. Squabbling pheasants took off as Ruscoe neared. A stream flowed by with its fast waters chattering, leaping with spurts over lichen-covered rocks, and meandering in rivulets over and about the polished pebbles. Ruscoe hurried across to it. Laying on his belly, he dipped his cupped hands in. He scooped up and drank furtively at first. The water was cool and unadulterated and so he supped greedily. He was glad of it and set off, in the direction of which the water ran, with hope and replenished vigour.

For an hour he trekked through the forest, following the stream; occasionally needing to skirt a gregarious collection of trees or wade into carpets of ground ivy, other times paddling through the water.

In the frenetic rush of city existence and dedication given to his work, Ruscoe had become isolated and regardless of other responsibilities. Yet here within the slow, breathing forest he was forced to confront himself, a timeless mirror reflecting back to him all that he was. Memories of himself and Sarah showed themselves and he was saddened, and hurt by them. These recollections highlighted his shortcomings and so, by shuffling through all the negative aspects of his personality, he had eventually reduced himself to a disgusting, despicable rogue. Was it possible he could be as villainous as the portrait he had constructed? He realised that being selfish and self-centred had alienated him from his wife, his friends and even his true self. Ruscoe resolved to make amends, once he was back home. It was never too late to change, to pay recompense, to mature and evolve…

The stream disappeared into the earth, below a contorted trunk astride a bank of crumbling chalk. Beyond was a mass of trees and bushes as impenetrable as a wall.

'No!' he shrieked. Without pause, he whipped around and stalked back against the flow of the stream, kicking it like a sulking child, splashing and sliding on the slippery stones. If this smug forest would not let him out one way, he would go the other. His patience was being pushed to the limit.

Despite possessing an all-encompassing weariness, Ruscoe was strangely exhilarated. Perhaps it was the absence of car fumes and the brisk exercise, with his lungs filled with clean air. Maybe this forest was not such a bad place after all. He had grown invisible blinkers over the years, he knew. Of course, the geometry and mathematics of the natural world could be as absorbing, its biochemistry as complex, as any microprocessor. He noted the foliage, admitting it was intriguing as the infinite patterns of a Fractal. With an eyeglass set upon a leaf, the fine tracery of its skeleton would become clear; then through a microscope, the pod-like stomata would be viewed in fascinating arrangements. One could investigate elements of one cell, then its molecules, and further onward into a microcosm of atoms, containing the subatomic particles; and smaller still to minuscule pulses of power, existing for a trillionth of a mere blink of an eye.

And what of the Theory of Chaos, which states that many physical attributes of nature and the development of all living things could be shown to abide by the function of a single, simple equation? One could almost believe in an elemental force which was responsible for the beautifully uncomplicated concept. Theological notions clattered in his mind.

A fox, warily twitching its brush, turned to an auburn statuette and fixed its attention upon the stranger before vanishing. This was enough to break Ruscoe's reverie and he thrust his head forward so that he might catch sight of the creature. Instead, he saw the distinctive misshapen boot of the abandoned vehicle.

This car seemed to be the hub of his existence, for no matter which way he went, he was doomed to come across it again sooner or later. No less than a nightmare, never-ending roundabout of events; whereupon reaching the end of them, he would revert to the beginning to relive the dreadfulness.

Ruscoe decided to rest before embarking on the journey upstream. After all, there was no point in rushing: it seemed the more he did so, the more the living forest played games with him. He hacked through the bushes with a stick to reach the car.

Although he was loath to admit, there might have to be another night spent away from habitation. Ruscoe began in earnest to empty the steel husk of its rubbish. He dumped the black bags in a pile away from this makeshift encampment. Once cleared, he discovered a sheet of olive tarpaulin spread over the floorpan, serviceable apart from oil stains and mildew. Woodlice and centipedes scuttled away as he dragged it out. Upon tying two ends to the window bars of the car, he supported the other side with some stout poles of wood pushed into the ground before clearing the area under the shelter. He hunted for dry branches and placed them methodically in a pile ready for a fire. He was easily exhausted and so lay down under the protection of the tarpaulin to rest for a while.

Ruscoe entertained himself by inspecting the discarded lumps of metal from out of the engine, imagining new uses for them or considering their original purpose. Then he collected some sticks and pebbles to devise an ingenious game of patience. Unexpectedly, he began to enjoy this relaxation. These pastimes did not require a deadline and his thought processes seemed clear in this arboreal setting. He was certain now he had been premature about his view of the countryside. After tiring of his game, he retrieved a penknife from the rucksack and set about stripping a branch of its bark. The smooth knurled shape appealed to him: resembling a writhing snake, he whittled at it to make it more so.

Ruscoe would close his eyes for a while before opening them to continue his handiwork. Eventually he succumbed and slipped into a delicious doze. The canopy trapped the moist, warm air heated by the glaring sun. He wriggled and turned under it, now and then gaining consciousness to scratch urgently or wipe his itching face before slipping back into a feverish sleep. He had been swallowing and taking from his mouth what he had thought to be – in delirious waking moments – crumbs of dirt. But a particularly sharp pricking sensation to his tongue caused him to open his inflamed eyelids. To his horror, he beheld a legion of ants teeming over him. They had found their way into his hair, clothes and nostrils, giving minute nips to his legs and swollen tongue. What had seemed a convenient grassy mound for laying his head was a red ants nest. Shuddering with horror and patting himself furiously, he turned over to see thousands more incarnadine specks streaming from it. He leapt to his feet with a yell, still smacking and shaking himself, revulsion enveloping him from the repulsive sensation of the crawling insects. In desperation, he barged through the bushes and trees, yanking away his clothes as he went. He threw his pale, wasted nakedness into the stream. The coldness of it took his breath away as he splashed and rolled in the cool water.

After dressing, then drinking to soothe his parched gullet, Ruscoe staggered along the stream, blaspheming and spluttering condemnation. He warned the forest of his desire for revenge: how he wished for the spirits instilled in wood and plant to shrivel so that without this fundamental force to bind together the ecosystem, it would wither and decay. Or that he would hire a bulldozer to clear the ground — or better still, set fire to it.

But first he must get out…

He gave a dry, mirthless titter. The dead end that Ruscoe surveyed was of no surprise: he had almost expected it. A broad lake stretched before him with waterhoppers skittering on it and translucent-winged dragonflies hovering over the water. Emerald pads of water lilies floated in clusters, waxy-cream flowers decorating them. Rushes and grasses fringed the perimeter. Alder, flecked with white lichen, relaxed there. Feathery willow hung their branches into it, gazing with contemplation at their own reflections and that of the sun that sparkled on its surface. Ducks dipped their beaks, breaking the lake's smoothness, rippling circles radiating out from them.

At any other time, even Ruscoe might have appreciated this for its beauty. But all poetic notions were far away, too busy was he contemplating the vicious wilderness which should wish to incarcerate him. For not only was the forest impenetrable either side of the lake with its densely packed undergrowth but, at the far end, gushes of white water cascaded from ledge to ledge of a vertical, angular rock-face. High up in clefts were untidy nests. The sound of gulls squabbling there was lost to the roar of the waterfall. Ruscoe was dispirited and he stayed long by the water's edge, sullen and tired.

Aims and ambitions seem pointless when one is faced with survival. He must find food. With plans of escape and retribution swamping his senses, he had not realised the abundance available. Now, with this prerequisite in mind, Ruscoe discerned sources of sustenance wherever he looked. A crab apple tree boldly displayed its fruit yet earlier he had walked passed it. He knocked down a number with a lean branch. Gingerly avoiding the spiny growths of blackberry bushes, he took their fruit; and even stole a speckled egg from a nest. He laid the pickings carefully into his backpack. The best find was a giant puffball – almost nine inches in diameter – which he had gently lifted from its root before cradling it proudly in his arms back to the abandoned car. He had read somewhere it could be consumed without worry.

His trophies were laid on the ground. He ate a few of the green apples and was surprised at how edible they were, though sharp to the palate, followed by a handful of blackberries crammed into his mouth. He would save the fungus and egg for later, he decided, once the fire was lit.

Already it was early evening. The sky was furnished with puffs of pink cloud and a feint moon. He must prepare for the night. Another day tomorrow: he was sure to escape then.

Ruscoe erected the tarpaulin on the other side of the metal carcass. Before being satisfied, he stamped upon the ground as if some archaic dance to ensure there were no more insect nests. Then he tore open the rubbish bags, one by one. The first bag was stuffed with newspaper but there was some twine he put aside. The second contained rotten refuse. After sorting through paint and food tins, crumpled clothes, bottles and broken crockery from the remainder, he had salvaged some useful items: a china mug, a metal bowl, a chipped plate and even an axe head and a fork. He washed them in the stream. Shielded by the canopy from the ever-weakening sunshine, he inspected them thoroughly. These would see him in good stead.

But what was he doing? Already he was acting as if he were staying. He was tricking himself — he must not be here anymore.

Again, the fighting through the verdant forest was useless. To keep a straight line was impossible and the few footpaths he came across took him to dead ends. And when coming upon the rusting hulk again, Ruscoe fell down with despair. The situation was preposterous: how could he be trapped in the English countryside, with villages, towns and people only a few miles away? The overgrown shrubbery was taunting him.

So, if another night must pass here, then at least he must do something useful. Ruscoe spent time pulling up weeds, and washing the inside of the car of its dirt and flaking rust before scrubbing it dry with rags. He cleared the site of stones and bracken, and broke up clods of earth to level it.

An idea came to mind: upon jamming a stick into the blunt axe head, he went to the stream to sharpen it on a wet stone. It took a long time but he was pleased with the results. He found a suitable branch – supple and tapering – which he chopped down and stripped of its offshoots. Attaching the twine to the thin end and an opened paperclip from his pocket to the twine, his rod and line was complete. He was going to catch a fish.

Ruscoe lingered by the lake until sunset – the golden rays tingeing the rippling surface – impatient for a fish to bite. He rubbed his stubbly chin: there were certainly some here for he had seen strings of bubbles rising, and catfish flapping between the rushes. He had tried blackberries for bait then a sandwich crust but they had merely nosed it or nibbled at it. Not until he had tried a wild plum did he have success. There was a satisfying tugging on the line and, with a whoop of excitement, he snatched out a carp with its glistening scales turned gold by the sun.

The flames were greedy as the fire crackled and flickered brightly. Ruscoe was comforted in his halo of light: a protective yellow globe keeping the deeper shadows at bay. It lit up the trees and made a prancing shadow play.

He squeezed some juices from the fish into his saucepan and fried the leathery steaks of the puffball before ramming a stick through the belly of the carp to toast it.

Ruscoe ate with relish and curiosity: he had not eaten a fish so fresh before; certainly he had never partaken of this particular fungus. The carp was disappointing for it tasted muddy, although he found the puffball enjoyable with its delicate flavour of sweetbread and texture of marshmallow. The meal was finished with blackberries, and cups of hot water flavoured with fruit juice.

He retired under the canopy and sleepily gazed at the dying flames and embers, and the flitting moths attracted by its light; and listened to the rasping of grasshoppers.

For seven days more he attempted to find the edge of the forest. Glades of oak and wild cherry in valleys led him to hazel and rambling hawthorn, then onto hills spread with pine — but the forest would not let him out. His nights were spent sleeping amongst dock leaves or on banks of moss. One evening, espying a badger set, he was forced to sleep curled in the bosom of a tree. While walking the next morning, he had inadvertently stumbled upon his camp again.

On the fifteenth day, Ruscoe scratched fifteen lines on the boot of the car. The inside of it was his larder — nuts and berries, barbel and tench wrapped in damp newspaper, and a variety of eggs. There was a collection of fungi: parasol mushrooms, ceps and shaggy inkcaps amongst others. He had learned that these rise from the earth overnight in dank and dark places and had become adept at finding the strange growths. He had tried eating acorns but found the raw kernels bitter. Roasting them as a side dish to trout was palatable. As a delicacy, he would fetch peppery watercress and tubers of the waterlily from the lake. He infused mulberry leaves and berries to make tea. The rod, left overnight with its line trailing into the water, would often have a catch the next morning, although Ruscoe would occasionally go fishing for relaxation.

He missed the taste of meat and so set about building a box trap. The rabbit caught under it was fortunate to be let free shortly after. Ruscoe had put his hands about its throat but quivering more than the animal in his grasp, he had begun to stroke its shivering fur as if it were a cat. If only the animal was already dead, skinned and wrapped in plastic.

Each day brought with it a new skill. He built a cabin with three sides set against the car body to include a door and window. It was fabricated from large branches set into the earth and bound with rope made from wiry rushes.

With the apparent uselessness of his treks – persuaded and cajoled always back to the encampment – Ruscoe's policy was to try every fourth day only. It was quite useless, he knew, but he must make the effort all the same.

Ruscoe swam in the lake and ran wherever he was able. He enjoyed the pure air and the freedom of his new lifestyle. He was exhilarated by sunsets, and the sighting of a creature or plant not seen before. He noticed climate changes: a blistering heat one day, or overcast the next; a light shower or a brisk breeze. And he learned the distinguishing features of many trees, wild flowers, animals and insects living there. He began to draw and catalogue them in his notepads; and if he did not known the name of a particular component of the flora and fauna, he would devise one of his own.

The weather turned mild. Ruscoe had washed the old clothes found in the rubbish bags several times and they soon lost their musty smell. After stitching them together with twine using the shard of a flint as a needle, the makeshift covers were more than adequate to keep out the cold evenings. Ruscoe would often jog through the forest on his quest for the perimeter, enjoying the brisk air and the exercise. As winter approached, he had almost given up hope of ever escaping. While the snow laid its crisp white blanket over everything, he did not venture too far and busied himself making a stove, complete with a smoke flue, manufactured from engine parts from the old car. He ensured the cabin was watertight by applying strips of leather cut from the car seats and plastic from the bags to its roof. It had been a wise precaution, for the spring brought with it heavy downpours of rain and hail.

Ruscoe was thrilled to watch the dormant trees and plants come alive again: the pastel shades of blossom, and the varied berries and flowers. And the return of so many birds, including a thrush which he was certain he had fed the year before. The reborn summer arrived finally. It seemed as hot as the previous season, if not more so.

Ruscoe's beard had grown thick and his long hair had regained its brown colour. He felt strong — not only in body but also in mind. From despising the forest, he had grown to respect it for the beauty there; the interest of the involved food-chain with its cycle of living and dying. He would talk to trees in hushed tones, telling them of plans in his life, or to lay bare worries, invoking and communing with their transcendental spirits.

What secrets were still to be uncovered: what manner of extraordinary things were there to be found? Grateful to his habitat for providing him his simple needs, Ruscoe vowed to give back to the earth. One must give to be able to take, but when would the world realise, he thought, before it's too late? It was as clear as the day now: the rape of the forests, the polluting of seas with chemicals and plastic, the wilful slaughter of wildlife — all of these devastating actions will eventually destroy us, if continued. Steps have to be taken now to arrest the humiliating destruction before the irreversible decline begins. Holes in the ozone layer cannot be patched – he mused – rainforests cannot be restored to the barren dusty plateaus, animals cannot be reconstituted; all evolved over billions of years to be eradicated by man's craving for power and money. Industry and commerce must have a conscience and accountability. Science must not be in a vacuum, divorced from reality, Ruscoe considered; we are a complicated, organic and inorganic whole whereby, like in the mechanism of a watch, every part depends on each other part.

He stood naked at the edge of the lake. The sun – life force for all living things – filled his every cell with joy. Blood ran vigorously in him. His sight had become acute and keen, and his once shabby, tired body transformed to being taught and upright, with bronzed muscles defined and strong. Preparing to dive, he paused. Ruscoe rejoiced in his nakedness. He breathed deeply the air and he glowed with dynamism and energy. Anguish and stress had been banished for ever as he rejoiced in a union with nature, an explosive vision of profound completeness; of joining with the very essence of creation. He swam as adroitly as a porpoise for half an hour. Then, hidden behind the waterfall on a slab of granite, he appreciated the sun's rays and mused on his sublime experience.

That evening, he kept the fire alight from the store of wood accumulated over many weeks, almost depleting it. Though he did not care: he wished to spend the night awake. He had made a genuine pact with nature which deserved his selfless attention and giving. He cherished every aspect of this true relationship; even the cloud of gnats hovering over stinging nettles; bluebottles crawling over the fish bones; the over-ripe fruit beginning to blister with decay.

The following afternoon, Ruscoe caught a pheasant in his box trap. He expertly broke its neck with a snap of the spine and immediately began to pull feathers from it, the wings still flapping furiously. Eventually the bird became still. He would save the feathers for another pillow. The deed was carried out without shame or remorse, for he knew man is a carnivore and therefore no different from a jaguar which stalks and kills its prey. Still we are different, Ruscoe considered whilst gutting and cleaning the insides of the meat; we hoard chickens bundled in cages, some blind with their eyes scratched out; or calves never to see daylight so that their albino flesh can be a lust for the appetite; and we mercilessly maim and kill our own kind with a sort of madness…

Ruscoe ate the roasted pheasant with plums, nettles and dandelion leaves.

After letting the meal digest, he set about tidying and cleaning the cabin. He looked forward to his chores for it gave him pleasure to view his creations. There was the table and stool carved from a single piece of timber. Shelves lined a wall, with interesting ornaments of crystal and root upon them, beeswax candles and course booklets of paper. He had discovered – quite by chance – that newspaper, steeped in water and the sap of a particular plant, was bleached so as to leave only feint remains of the ink. Two car seats with their backs broken made as good a bed as any. Sprays of wild rose stood in pots and bouquets of fragrant flowers hung from the rifted walls. A picture hung there also, made from shells and pebbles embedded into clay.

The solution of how to find his way out of the forest had come in a dream. He was annoyed that he had not devised it in his waking hours. He had dreamt he was carving trunks into totems, and daubing them with weird glyphs and runes. Upon awakening, Ruscoe had immediately hurried to the rubbish pile to sort out the paint tins. Prising the lid from one he had found oily fluid laying on a paint crust. After stirring it thoroughly and preparing the others in the same manner, there was more than enough paint for his enterprise.

Each time Ruscoe ventured out over the following week,

he would paint a number with a direction arrow on a tree at regular intervals. Upon his return he would apply this new knowledge to a map. When trying a new route and coming across a sign on the bark, he was able to mark where the ways crossed and intersected. With the stream, lake and car drawn at the epicentre of all this, the map was almost complete.

One particularly warm morning, Ruscoe had finished scratching another line on the boot of the car when he decided to count them. With an eyebrow raised, he gave a chuckle. Today was the anniversary of his stay in the forest: today was the three hundred and sixty sixth day.

Later on, Ruscoe sat at the table to update the map. He was drawing thick curves of graphite on it to indicate the journey he had taken that morning, whereupon he stared in astonishment. This was the final piece of the puzzle. Tracing the lines and curves with a finger, Ruscoe checked and re-checked the validity of them, like a physicist who has discovered a unique set of equations, not daring to believe what he saw. It was extraordinary how he had avoided obvious routes and incredible that he had missed opportunities or repeated the same mistakes over and over. But there it was on the page as conspicuous as if written in large phosphorescent letters: the way out.

Ruscoe cleared the larder and threw the contents into the bushes, and put his diary and a few mementoes into his backpack. He poured earth on hot ashes still smouldering from the night before and, without looking back, set off.

Adrenaline coursed through him: he was excited and expectant. He rushed (as one is encouraged to by a city) as if late for work. Indeed, several times he caught himself looking to his watch strapped again to his wrist.

Astounded, Ruscoe discovered his bike where he had left it twelve months before. Following the advice from his map, he chose to ignore the way he had come those months ago and cut across instead, a difficult task being encumbered with a bicycle. Not very far through the forest, he discovered the piles of cut trunks and uprooted trees. He leapt on his bike and so strong was he now, he picked up an extraordinary speed along the forest path.

And there was the meadow. Ruscoe sprinted between the trees, and tripped into the open as if the forest had said: "Go then if you must! Leave me quickly!" The strong sunlight lit his hirsute face. He stroked the beard and shook his head in consternation. The model aeroplanes still played high in the air, slicing it with their growls; the brown dog still ran through the gorse, and a magpie chased its mate out from under a thorny bush.

Ruscoe inspected the watch. The second hand – showing six-thirty – twitched into movement again. The watch glass glinted. Across the other side of the meadow, Sebastian stood beckoning by the Waterside Inn and raising a glass of ale to the sun.

Ruscoe unstrapped the watch with dedicated ceremony and flung it into the brambles.

His mission was certainly clear; he was not ready to leave. There was more to learn, more significance and understanding to be bestowed upon him.

He turned back. Walking slowly into the arms of the forest, Ruscoe Robinson smiled.

There was firewood to be fetched.

THE HIDDEN LIBRARIES OF DOCTOR DANCER

Mausoleum Park is a neglected public space. It could have once boasted colonnades and lawn terraces, a windmill, tea rooms, and hemmed by grand private houses with sweeping terraces and exquisite lawns. Or so we are led to believe by the few local history books which have recorded the origination and eventual passing of the park and its attendant houses.

One fact which cannot be known for sure is the origin of the name. Many theories have been put forward as to why the area was a park at all, and the true meaning of the word Mausoleum. The majority of professional knowledge and opinions of its mysterious history tend to agree there was never such an edifice built on those acres; and if there had been, it was destroyed without any historical record.

To a degree, this is not surprising because a terrace of those marvellous old Victorian houses, described as having turrets, wings and ornate tiling, also vanished overnight. Let me underline here, I'm not meaning in any literary sense but in a literal sense: one day they were there, the next, not; just empty space, not even basements left behind, or foundations of any sort.

The Windrock Borough Council tried their best for a few years to keep it clear of overgrowth, as well as the rougher elements who seemed to congregate amongst the network of muddy pathways between the trees. A friend of mine told me a while ago that there were dens hidden somewhere for those thieves and murderers although I take that with a pinch of salt.

So it has become a park again over the past couple of years, with large areas cleared with just meadow left, wooden walkways and stream bridges built where needed, and the Clocktower Tea Rooms open again for business. The area is popular, mainly in the spring and summer months, attracting families out for the day for a bit of fresh air, dog walkers, kite flyers, metal detectors, and botanists, like myself.

It has become an all-encompassing hobby of mine of late, especially as I recently moved into a terraced house not even half a mile away from the park. It's easy, on my days off, to cycle there, chain the bike up at the tearooms and ramble through the woods in search of interesting plant specimens, especially found near the ponds and streams – the damp and humid places. It was while cycling in one of those particularly dense areas, not far from the clearing where the vanished house used to stand, that I discovered a book. It was lodged in a tree, approximately fifteen feet up. The find certainly looked intriguing and I was keen to retrieve it from its grasping branches.

I ascertained that even by standing on the saddle of my bicycle, there wasn't any way to start a climb into the tree. But then, finding a decent stick, at least five feet long, I managed to balance on the saddle after all, with the bicycle leaning on that thick trunk of a tree. By hugging the tree, and reaching up with the stick, I was able to knock the strange find to the ground.

Upon opening the book's hardback cover, I found the pages to be blank, and inset was an ornate door key; at least, I assumed it was for a door. I placed the find in my jacket pocket, mounted my bicycle, and headed for the track which leads to the area of the vanished houses.

To my astonishment – and I mean astonishment – there was the row of Victorian houses, their tons of weight definitely planted on the earth where they used to be before simply vanishing.

The house in the middle had wrought iron railings and consisted of three stories, six windows on each storey. A flight of concrete steps led to a pair of ornately carved double doors, one of which opened. A man dressed in a smart but antique suit immediately beckoned to me.

This solid phantom of a man spoke with a cultured and deep voice, 'Welcome to libraries of Doctor Dancer.'

I spoke the first thought which came to mind.

'Are you a guide?'

'Indeed I am not,' he replied. 'You shall be your own guide.' And with that said, he held out a slim hand. I leant my bicycle against the railings and mounted the steps. I went to shake his hand though I didn't know why I should; and he retracted it, and I did likewise, feeling puzzled. Not only for the stranger's retraction but for the reason I had felt compelled to shake the hand in the first place.

Again he extended an arm, but this time with his pale palm turned upwards.

'I'm not understanding,' I remember remarking. But then it dawned on me, perhaps this unusual man wanted the key I had found in the tree.

I searched in my jacket pocket and retrieved the key, placing it into the man's palm with a sort of reverence, as though it were part of some esoteric ritual.

The moment I did so, the other side of the door opened and a young man, staring wildly at me, stood swaying on the top step.

'Sorry,' he muttered before running down the steps before running towards my bicycle leaning against the railings. He looked very familiar.

I was distracted by the besuited gentleman going back inside the house and he said, 'This way.'

After a moment of hesitation, I followed.

Silence then. Utter and complete silence. The man was nowhere to be seen.

I found myself in a large hallway with a huge, sweeping staircase in the middle leading to the next floor, though at the top was a brick wall. All surfaces, apart from the stairs and brick wall, and a door to the left and the ornately-designed floor tiles, were covered in mirrors.

My reflection each side went on to infinity.

'Hello,' I called out. I walked over to the door on the left and tried it but it was locked.

A dream state within reality, I considered then, especially as the chandelier descended behind me with a grating of its chain, and when it was at eye-level, there was another small book within its pendants, identical to the one I had found in the woods; and inside an identical key. I retrieved it and tried it in the door. It fitted. I unlocked the door and opened it, stepping through to a large room. Ornate coving along three sides. A mottled ceiling and flock wallpaper on two of the walls. The third wall was panelled. Dark oak or possibly mahogany, some of the panels scratched. And the fourth wall was covered with bookcases, holding antique books, their spines gold impressed and chiselled.

I took one of the volumes from its shelf and opened it. The pages were blank. As were any other book I chose to extract to inspect.

For a moment, sense returned and I felt I must leave the silent room. I opened the door through which I had come in, back to the hallway. At least, I would have naturally assumed it would take me back to the hallway. Instead, I stepped into an identical room to the one I had left behind. Except there were bookcases on two sides and the room could be seen to be even larger.

Compelled again to inspect these books, though this time with multi-coloured spines – I found they could not be opened, each book made solid as if carved from glued paper.

How many more times did I go through that same door to identical rooms, each room becoming larger than the next? How many times did I look at the books on the bookcase shelves in each? I can't recall.

Though I do remember the volumes in each: projections of books, books made from stale cake, those volumes with the inside text printed upside down, those in a language like nothing on earth, those with cryptic symbols, enigmatic diagrams; books in one room each with its own fragrance; tiny books, books more than 10 feet high on only one shelf, reaching to the ceiling; books made from candle wax, powdered horses' hooves and other exotic materials; rare metals and alloys.

I entered the final room, for I knew this to be final. Looking back to the door, it had vanished, and there weren't any bookcases, just four walls half-panelled and papered with flock wallpaper, and a spiral staircase at one side of it.

I trod up the staircase, trepidation in my step, hoping there might be a way of escape above. At the top of the staircase, I found a casement window, overlooking the edge of Mausoleum Park. On the windowsill lay another book with a key shape cut out inside. I placed the door key there. Through some impulse, I opened the window, with the idea I could climb out but realised I was on the second floor.

I was in a dream state. My instinct told me to throw the book with the key inside through the open window, as hard as I was able. It flew across to the trees at the Mausoleum perimeter and lodged in a tree.

I stood for a while looking at the scene framed by the casement window as if it were a painting, then trod back down the spiral staircase to the empty room again. Though this time, the staircase continued through the floor to a room below, identical to the first room I had visited, the one with the antique volumes held on their dark wood shelves.

I hurriedly pulled the door open and walked back out into the mirrored hallways.

The besuited gentleman stood with his back to the brick wall at the top of the staircase, before gently padding down the carpeted stairs.

I watched with a type of fascination, as if he moved within

a dream. He walked in a formal fashion to the double doors and opened the right hand one. While in conversation with someone on the doorstep, I took the opportunity to escape, flinging open the left hand door.

Had my experience been no more than a circus or fairground illusion, without meaning; or were there hidden deeper metaphysical traits yet to be uncovered, from their influence on my mind? In a way it didn't matter as I yelled to the new visitor, 'Sorry,' and rushed down the granite steps and over to my bike still leaning against the railings.

Author's note: after finding this story handwritten in the drawer of my sideboard, I can safely say I have no recollection of writing it; nor have I any memory of its events happening in a dream world or in reality.

One thing is certain though. I shall be visiting the tree in Mausoleum Park tomorrow to see if I can find that key within the book lodged in its branches.

MOBILE

'We've been sent on a wild goose chase,' Pico said.

The town centre was empty of people. Parked cars sat in lines along side roads awaiting their owners. A sharp morning sun attempted to penetrate the shadows which the buildings made. There were empty café tables, some with half-drank coffee there, the pavements clear of pedestrians. Pigeons had taken the opportunity to congregate. An unusual quietness enveloped the air.

Pico and Jim looked to each other; Pico shrugged. Looking through the window of a supermarket, they saw the rows of checkout tills, a few assistants sat at their stations, gazing blankly or chatting.

A man came out of a shop, carrying a shopping bag.

Jim asked, 'Hey, morning to you. Is Sandsville normally this quiet?' His dark features became animated with a smile.

The stranger looked at him as though not understanding the question.

'It's the new gadget, third wave.'

'Sure, we understand that, but where is everybody?'

'New gadget, third wave, I just told you.' The man looked slightly annoyed and began to walk away.

Pico called after him.

'But the event: empty in the Civic Centre.'

He looked over to the building in question.

The man turned.

'Venue changed; Town Hall now. Suppose I'm not meant to tell but everyone else knows.'

'That explains how we got a car space so close to the Civic Centre,' Pico said under his breath then aloud, 'they can't all be at the Town Hall, can they? Why aren't you there? And can you tell us where the Town Hall is?'

'You sure have a lot of questions,' the man answered. 'I don't need no gadgets; and the Town Hall is two blocks that-a-way.' He pointed across the street.

Pico looked to Jim before crossing the empty road, wading into the pigeons, sending them flapping into the air. He sat at one of the street tables outside of a café. Jim hurried up to him and said, 'Hadn't we better get going, Pico? We've only got half an hour or less before…'

A waiter had walked swiftly out of the café entrance and up to Pico, a notepad and pencil in his hand. 'What can I get you?'

Pico answered, 'Thanks, but I'm just making a call. Alright to sit here?' and he extracted his magenta-coloured mobile from a pocket.

The waiter shook his head and gave a look of disapproval before turning to walk back to the café. But then, catching sight of the mobile, he stopped.

'Where you at?' he said with a grin. He bent to inspect the mobile in Pico's hand more closely, then his grin dropped. 'Never mind,' he muttered before walking swiftly away.

'What did he mean by that?' Jim asked.

'He thought my mobile was a Domane. All will be explained later, as I told you,' replied Pico to his colleague.

'OK. Now if you're phoning work, can I suggest you talk on the move otherwise we'll be late. I'm keen to see what this is all about.' Pico nodded and once he had the dial tone, he stood. Jim started to walk, expecting Pico to follow. 'Come on, we don't want to miss the event.'

'Hi, Jade? Pico. The venue's been changed.'

Jade stood in a third floor office of the Lightman Telecommunications Institute, gazing over the campus, its red brick research buildings scattered over the ten acre site as if at random, slim roads snaking around them.

'I could have told you that,' she answered.

Pico laughed but still with modest vexation.

'Then why didn't you?'

Jade ignored the question and said, 'For some reason, all the venues were changed at the last minute – Hillingdon, Waterson, Hainbury and the rest.'

Jim started to walk with Pico following behind.

'And here in Sandsville too; the event is in the Town Hall. OK, we're on our way now.'

As Pico entered an arcade of shops strung along a wide alley, a man, haggard in features although dressed in an expensive suit and tie, was loping towards him.

He stopped now and then to bellow into shop doorways, 'The next number!'

He appeared deeply agitated and his strange eyes swivelled as he clutched his head.

Pico kept his sight on the nervous man and continued to

Jade, 'Did you contact the Research Facility on the campus? If we get hold of—'

The strange character was in front of Pico now and a hand shot out to grasp the mobile, pulling it to him, and his other shaking hand pushed hard onto Pico's chest. And as Pico lost balance and was sent to the ground, the man screamed, 'Il numero, het aantal, die Zahl, le nombre, the number, the next number, the number!' He held the mobile at arm's length, shouting, 'Please Peter – Aaron – Nathan – Comforter – stop with the next number, stop–' It was then his grey eyes from his grey face seemed to focus; his arm fell to his side and with his shoulders slumped, he dropped Pico's mobile and fell against a wall, his head hanging down.

'Hey you,' Jim said. 'What do you think you're playing at?'

Pico had picked up his mobile and got to his feet.

'Leave it, Jim,' he said.

The distraught man was mumbling.

'I'm two…the number; what's the next number, next number…'

'But he's just attacked you.'

Look,' Pico said, 'you go to the event. Here's Manfred's pass card. I'm going to stay here with this guy.'

'Let's leave it, he'll be alright; the Town Hall is only a couple of blocks away.'

'What's number three?' the man said as if to himself, his eyes now glazed again.

Pico studied the man with concern, and pulled Jim across to the other side of the alley. He spoke quietly.

'He's just like Manfred before he died. It's something to do with the third phase. I'm going to stay to see if I can help.'

'Pico, you've got to tell me more of what's going on.'

'I told you, my friend Macca will explain better. It could be dangerous otherwise – for both of us.'

'What do you mean by that?'

'You'll understand when you meet Macca. I'll phone him now.'

'How will I find Macca?'

'You won't. He'll find you. I've shown him your photo, he knows what you look like. So go, and I'll see you back at the Institute.'

'Well, if you're sure,' Jim said.

'Sure I'm sure.'

Jim bade farewell to Pico and continued along the alley. He turned back to see him leaning on a brick wall next to the disturbed man, a hand on his shoulder, talking to him.

Turning left into another main road, a few pedestrians scurried past with worried looks upon their faces, glancing suspiciously at Jim. There was an unusual barrage of noise from the next street, sounding like waves breaking or a moderate wind.

Reaching the end of the road, he turned right and continued, following the source of the sound. A young woman hurried up to him and Jim, expecting an attack similar to that of Pico's, took a step back. But she merely looked downcast and murmured, 'you won't get in.'

The further Jim walked, the louder the noises became until just before reaching the town's square, he recognised them – people shouting and squabbling, crying out; a babble of voices.

And upon turning the corner, he was confronted with the

source: hundreds of people cluttering the square. And if it was not for the angry faces and banners, one could almost believe it was a festival. Still, some had taken the opportunity of the moment: a four-piece jazz band played under cover of a shop awning and street hawkers wove their way between the groups. The main knot of people were jammed together outside, near the stone steps of the Town Hall, jeering and waving their banners.

The closer Jim got to the steps, the more difficult it was to push his way through. A line of light grey-suited bodyguards stood on the steps leading to the main entrance. They grimaced and stared impassionately ahead, as if their attitude was enough to keep the crowd from advancing. But strangely, apart from one or two at the front who made a half-hearted attempt to get through – easily repelled by one of the guards – the majority stood in place, shouting and swearing.

Jim had managed to get to no more than six metres away from the Town Hall entrance but to get any further was an impossibility. Then an idea struck him: if he were to wave the pass at one of the guards, perhaps he would be shown a clear passage through. He fumbled in his pocket and extracted the plastic pass, and was about to raise it above his head when his arm was held in a tight grip. The man with long hair tied into a ponytail, dressed in black, did not lessen the pressure of his hand.

'Don't do that,' an American voice commanded quickly.

'Why not?'

'Think about bodies trampled into concrete and faces bloodied, and your arm wrenched from its socket, just to get that pass. Follow me.'

'No, I want to get into the Town Hall, to the event.'

'You, me and six hundred others here, pal. If you want to get in, follow.'

The man in black wove his way through the knots of people, gaining speed as the crowd thinned. Jim had trouble keeping up and lost him once or twice but finding shortcuts he was able to catch up.

The man had stopped ahead. Before him, blocking his way, were two thugs harassing him. The American was gesticulating and shrugging until one of his aggressors started to push him, and said, 'Pass, watch, wallet, all of it small guy.'

Then Jim heard his reply, slow and low, spoken through clenched teeth, 'Minus seventy.'

The aggressors put their hands up as if a gun were being pointed at them.

'Woah, we're out'a here,' one said and they disappeared into the crowd.

Jim wrinkled his nose.

'Minus seventy? What…'

'Shuddup!' the new acquaintance shouted.

'Look, I was only asking…'

The American interrupted again and smiling suddenly, spoke quietly. 'Hey, I don't know why it works. I discovered high ranking Satyr Corporation employees use the term, amongst others.' He held out a slim hand. 'Louis Macfie. Friends call me Macco.'

Jim shook hands and replied, 'Jim Dinne. So now why do you tell me to shut up? My mouth ripped off, I suppose.'

'Said to the wrong person? Something like that,' replied Macco. 'Let's get going.'

They walked to the end of the square and as they turned the corner, Jim asked, 'Tell me, how come if I have a low rez hologram of my colleague's friend's face and finger scan on the entry pass, people would still want it? Surely it'd be of no use to them, even if they could find the way in?'

Macco nodded knowingly.

'How did you expect to get in with someone else's pass?'

'For the third wave event of a truly revolutionary mobile device?'

'You're learning their lines well.'

'Going to explain I've come along in place of someone who's…'

'Dead?' Macco finished.

'I guess Pico told you that,' Jim said.

'I told Pico; whatever. As for explaining, there'll be no need – friends in the know tell me security is lax at entry points. Especially at the back here.' They were in a side street now, walking towards the large wrought iron gates barring the way to the rear of the Town Hall. There were still fifty or so people there but they seemed to be listlessly marching by, stopping to peer through the gates, then walking on, only to change direction to repeat the performance. 'Just copy me in attitude. Play dumb, confused. Shuddup now.'

They pushed their way easily to the front of the small throng. Only two grey-suited guards stood in front of the gate. Both wore a small circular pin badge. On it was a dark grey spiral on a green background.

'Do as I do,' Macca whispered. He withdrew his pass card and waved it in front of one of the guards, a silly grin lighting his pale face. 'Crazy for it!' he said, nodding his head.

Jim showed his card and said with urgency, 'What's the next number?' Macca lost his mirth for a moment and looked confused, then regained his inane smile as the guard nodded with a hint of derision about him. He clicked two fingers and one gate swung open, enough for both of them to walk through. They went across a paved courtyard, palm trees in large square containers in each corner.

Macca turned to check that the guards still had their backs to him then he gripped Jim's shoulders and stared intently into his eyes.

'Are you playing a game?' He held his mouth firmly.

Jim was surprised and caught off guard.

'Macca, I've only just met you; what sort of game would I be playing?'

Macca visibly relaxed and let go his hold but still looked hard at Jim.

'OK, I guess you learnt that from Man; you must know some of the problems with the first and second phases.'

'What man? What problems? Pico and I met this guy who tried to steal his mobile and he was saying it. That's all. Not that I understand what it means.'

'OK, pal.'

An official wearing a gold chain of office ushered them in through the wooden back door and exclaimed, 'Welcome! Recepción, Willkommen, Benvenuto!' His grey eyes were ringed with grey pads of puffed flesh.

'This guy I mentioned, same thing,' Jim said quietly.

'I know, shuddup,' Macca answered, smiling benignly to their host.

Once they had entered and crossed the small lobby, Macca

snapped, 'Stay here,' and ignoring two doors which were entrances to offices, he opened a third door and went through. Jim was confused and went to follow but decided to take Macca's advice and stay put.

He turned to look at one of the dark corners of the lobby, light from the stained glass window set high in the wall shunning it. There was a figure standing in that corner, he was certain, dressed in a dark grey robe, shifting from side to side, studying him.

He was turned firmly about. Macca had come back.

'Hey, what you doing now?' Jim asked, becoming annoyed.

'Move on and shuddup,' Macca said quickly.

As they walked down a wide corridor, past paintings of previous mayors in gilt frames on the walls, and large aerial photographs of Sandsville, Jim spoke with annoyance.

'All you do is keep telling me to shut up.'

'I do, don't I,' Macca answered without humour.

'So where did you go?'

'A hunch and I was right. There's stairs to underground offices. But also a door through to the side of the stage at the front.'

'You are becoming mighty mysterious, Macca. So what?'

'In case of trouble. Always good to add to your options for a quick exit.'

Jim shook his head.

'Trouble? Quick exit? I've a lot of questions to ask you,' he said.

'I know,' Macca replied succinctly. 'Then before we go in, let's talk first. Follow me.'

Jim followed him through the door and down the stairs to

the basement offices, and entered one. There was a conference table ringed by twelve chairs, with a white pen board on an easel and a slide projector to one side.

'Can we use this room?'

'Who says we can't?' Macca replied. 'Everyone's too excited and frantic upstairs to worry us. Anyhow, their fault for leaving the door unlocked.'

'Fair enough. I have to ask,' Jim said, 'Why are you helping me?'

'Because I want you to avoid what happened to Man.'

'Mankind? I don't understand.'

'If it continues to go the way it is, then mankind will need all the help it can get. No, I'm talking about Manfred.'

'Ah, of course, Pico's friend. You knew Manfred?'

'Yes. He was my brother.' Macca looked sullen. 'This so-called revolutionary device ruined his life and is ruining millions of other lives.' Then with a determined sigh added, 'It has to be stopped. No more deaths, no more suicides.'

'Manfred committed suicide?'

Macca looked angry. 'You told me you knew Manfred. How could you not know?'

'I don't mean to offend you,' Jim replied. 'As I said, your brother was Pico's friend. Pico has only told me so much. I never met Manfred. Not certain I understood Pico's vague explanation; never even seen one of the devices. How could such a thing cause so much upset?'

'Put simply, the first phase, the Domane One, had a holographic capability which projects a six by nine inch floating screen.'

'How could that cause problems?'

'In itself, none, other than a lust for the device. But also there is a system for fast-track language learning. The device can somehow scan your brain to allow for skilled learning of French or German, for instance, in a matter of days.'

'I remember Pico mentioning Manfred's abilities with other languages. But again I can't see any problems with that.'

'We're still trying to find out what technology is being used to scan the user because, afterwards, the person is not quite the same person they were. They act as if a drug addict, addicted to the device, addicted to the holographic images, especially in contact with someone called The Comforter; addicted to the speed-learning too, with friends reporting that the person may well speak another language fluently but use sentences they wouldn't otherwise have said themselves – as if they are being manipulated, used as a mouthpiece for another's mind.'

Jim frowned. 'That's far-fetched.'

'Listen, pal, my brother died through use of this evil device so don't you give me any more of your crap.'

'Hey, sorry, really. This is making sense now with the little that Pico told me. Please, tell me more. What was phase two?'

Macca continued, 'OK. Before I tell you, no more bad vibes, alright?' He drew in breath. 'Phase two, the Domane Two mobile, was released only a couple of months ago. And it's incredible what it can do if it wasn't so awful. By phoning another person who owns a Domain mobile, that person needn't use their mobile - they hear the call in their head.'

'Are you talking about telepathy?'

Macca nodded.

'And it's begun to drive some people nuts.'

'Why not just stop using it?'

'I told you, it's like a drug, the strongest drug you'll ever find. Anyway, even without their Domane on them, they still will hear another's voice inside them, sometimes more than one voice talking at a time. It's as though, by this initial brain scanning, something is put into their heads for their brains to become the mobile phone.'

'Pico told me the whole thing is crazy and I wouldn't believe him. So will the Domane Three offer any help?'

'There are rumours of phase three curing the problems. Who knows. Come on, let's get moving. It's going to kick-off soon.'

They came out of the office and up the stairs then along a corridor to the Town Hall main reception area. Outside, the sea of people seemed to be swaying, still blocked from advancing up the steps to the large glass fronted doors.

Turning sharply to their left, they were confronted by a steward standing next to a terminal on a plinth.

'Go through,' the official stated flatly.

Huddled rows of people stood lining the back of the hall as well as the sides, a human perimeter to the rows of those seated. The balconies were full and there was a hum of conversation. The majority of those seated seemed to be speaking to themselves, with haggard and grey faces.

Macca twitched his head as a sign for Jim to follow and they made their way behind the back standing group and along the side, finally stopping fairly close to the stage. Looking between the heads of those in front, Jim could see people standing in the aisles between the filled seating blocks.

Either side of the stage, in front of the curtains, stood placards showing large photographs of an object the shape of a mobile phone; an oblong with rounded corners, a dark magenta, but with no other visible attributes, not even a screen. It looked as if it could be no more than an unusually shaped and coloured pebble.

The rumble of voices came from expectant faces; a spontaneous clapping of hands came from somewhere in one of the galleries.

Jim spoke close to Macca's ear.

'So you used someone else's card?'

'The first phase was mobiles given to the heads of corporations,' Macca replied. 'Maybe there were cards scanned then, for security reasons. The second was to university and college professors and high profile celebrities. This third phase is to other key managers and workers, and maybe mopping up those missed from the first two phases. I'm trying to tell you, now the card system ain't worth a dime. They didn't even bother scanning our cards outside, did they.'

'So what's the point of them?'

'One word: hype. You saw the crowds outside. It's the same across the UK, America, Russia, you name it. Even changing the venue to a smaller one, helps to stoke the appetite of those who can't get in for a future phase.'

'I'm still not sure about this so-called technological marvel. I can't find any mention on the web yet you say the world is going nuts for them.'

'Some setup somewhere is trawling the web and blocking any mention of it. This has gotten crazy through cult following and word of mouth alone. The rumble in the jungle is that there'll be a fourth phase in no more than a couple of months time.'

Macca turned from Jim as vociferous applause greeted a man dressed in mayorial attire, who had walked onto the stage. He gave a theatrical bow and after waiting for the applause to subside, leant forward to a microphone on a stand in front of him. He smiled generously and spoke.

'Good afternoon, ladies and gentlemen, and welcome. As some of you know, I am the mayor of Sandsville and I'm most honoured to have been chosen to represent the Satyr Corporation, to explain more about their third phase. Thank you for watching the introductory video. As you saw, the marvellous and, may I say, unique mobile phone device I have been presented with is exactly the same as that of the second phase. But with a wonderful addition. I can now reveal the name of this addition to you. It's called…let me just read from my paper here – holographic mind meld. I have my device from the future … and soon so will you!'

A clamour of cheering, clapping and stamping feet erupted, and the mayor bellowed into the microphone, 'Ladies and Gentlemen, I give you – The Domane Three!' He held the device in the air for all to see, a projection of it showing large on the screen behind him. Most of those in their chairs rose to their feet still clapping and several tried to get closer to the stage but were stopped by more men in grey suits.

The applause died down and the mayor continued, 'By scanning your head with the Domane Three, as you did with the Domane Two, thus activating it, your new voice command available to you will be "hologram expanded". But before more explanation, I have a surprise for you. We are going to be distributing Domanes to you now, free of charge.' The place erupted again, the mayor shouting over the cacophony of voices, 'yes, that's right, if you'll all calm down we'll do just that.'

'This crowd is getting ridiculous,' Jim muttered.

All had taken their seats again and heads turned to stare at twenty or so men who had been standing in the aisles, wearing light grey robes, each holding a large cardboard box. They began to hand out Domane Threes, passed along the rows of seats and over to those standing. Robed figures were doing the same in the balconies.

'There's plenty there,' the mayor continued, 'plenty for everyone.'

Excited squeals, and happy conversation and laughter sprang up, those who had received their mobile studying it closely, some even kissing it.

'When everyone has their Domane Three, we'll start.'

After five minutes, the babble of excited voices calmed down and the mayor told them to scan and activate. This the crowd did as one, passing the device across their foreheads, and all spoke the word "hologram". Straight away, the holographic screen projection appeared on each of the mobile devices, hovering eight inches away, every one showing the new owner's head and shoulders.

'Now point your Modane to the stage area,' the mayor instructed. The audience turned their Modane Three's around as requested. 'And now the new command: hologram expanded,' said the mayor, and the multitude spoke the command together, sounding like the ending of a prayer.

All at once, the projected holographic images of each of their heads zoomed out and enlarged, to be seen projected onto the air in front of the stage with a size of at least fifteen feet wide and high. Each Modane owner's head and shoulders overlaid onto one another to form a composite holographic image: this one head and shoulders showing an androgynous face without hair, and eyes filled with black. The audience watched, as though hypnotised, with their grey eyes, grey faces and open mouths. The large composite image spoke and as it did so, every one of the new owners of the Domane Three spoke the same words at the same time, like a mantra: 'Welcome to hive consciousness. I am The Comforter.'

'What the…' Jim said but his voice was cut short as the double doors at the back of the hall swung open and a swarm of people ran through, pushing and shoving, taking Modanes from the hands of those who had received it, the composite image beginning to lose definition until vanishing all together. Shrieks and angry voices; squabbling and fighting beginning.

'The rabble outside must have got in!' Macca yelled amidst the shouts and commotion, as the milling crowd pushed him further into the centre of the hall.

Jim's head bobbed from side to side as he tried to follow Macca's unintentional progress towards one of the robed men. Strangely, those robed ones seemed calm and still, like grey beacons dotted throughout the thrashing waves of people. Macca now became totally separated from Jim as the crowds pushed and shoved their way to the main exits.

Then Macca shouted above the clamour, before becoming lost in the stampede, 'I'll be in contact. Get out of this madness.'

Jim threw his sight to his left, and there was the door at the side of the stage. He pushed and barged his way between the brawling crowd and once through, shut it behind him. He walked a couple of paces and looking up to the inside of the curtain on the stage, saw the mayor peeking through into the hall, fear engrained upon his features.

Jim made his way past a flight of steps and through another door and found himself in the lobby again.

He brushed himself down and ran to the back entrance. Glancing to his right, he thought that the shadows in the corners shifted; running out across the courtyard he was prepared for an argument with the guards but they were nowhere to be seen, so he went through the already-open wrought iron gates.

He wove his way through the few groups of people remaining and walked swiftly away from the area. After running to the end of the road, he turned a corner quickly and crossed to the other side of the street. A robed man had appeared, walking with swift steps as if gliding, a determined look upon his sharply defined features.

Jim felt a surge of panic rising within him. He ran into a winding side alley, past bow windows and clothes shops with gaunt mannequins. But then, running round a slight bend, he was confronted with a high wall.

He turned around to see the grey robed man, now walking slowly towards him, mouth curling and eyes unblinking.

Jim was no fighting man but in his fright, he brought his fists up as protection or even to throw a blow should it come to it.

The strange man stood in front of him now and one of his hands moved slowly to a grey bag held in place by the grey rope around his waist.

Jim was transfixed by the stranger staring – no whites to the robed man's eyes, just total black with no irises.

He was about to speak but then the robed one said in a casual fashion, 'You forgot this,' as he took a dark sculpted oblong from his bag. It was a Domane mobile phone.

He passed it across Jim's forehead before thrusting the device into Jim's hand.

Immediately, Jim felt warmth from the Domane Three. As he studied its perfectly smooth surface, the granulated colour evolved from one hue to another. He turned it over: it was featureless both sides. He looked up quickly to ask a question but the robed man had vanished.

And Jim heard words inside his head, distinct and encouraging, 'I am The Comforter. Let us talk.'

THE ULTIMATE SECRET

I glanced back to Aunt Adeline's ramshackle cottage before rushing out of the ivy-strangled garden and over to the car. I flung the door open, clambered into the seat, and grabbed the laptop. Now I am typing fast, so as not to forget any of the implausible story told me by that person claiming to be Aunt Adeline.

To start: my mother only told me recently that she has a sister, or rather had a sister, now believed to be dead. She explained her long-held anger at the rift between them for so many years, and sadness at not making amends before losing contact with her.

Intrigued, I decided I must track down her sister, to see if she still lived. After much online investigation, I visited the tucked-away village of Bartonham – the last-known location of Aunt Adeline – and spent the evening chatting with the locals in their creaky-beamed inn. And with my surreptitious investigation, I was finally told that my mother's sister is still alive, though a recluse of sorts, hiding herself away in Cherry Tree Cottage on the outskirts of the village.

I also learnt about Belinda, Aunt Adeline's home help, who cleans, cooks, and looks after her other needs.

So, on this misted early morning, I dared to force open the rotting front gate of Cherry Tree Cottage and walked along the diamond-tiled path and up to the rotting door. I rapped on it with the iron knocker, expecting an elderly lady to be appear, one with a variation of my mother's wrinkled features.

Instead, a smiling young woman opened the door. In her early twenties, I estimated, with the most lustrous hair I have ever seen, and beautiful clear skin on her cultured face and hands. She appeared angelic-like with almost an aura about her person. I asked her if the cottage was where Adeline lived. She told me in a dulcet tone that she was Adeline.

I retorted in an annoyed tone that she couldn't possibly be my aunt, because Adeline would be seventy-nine, possibly eighty years old.

Ignoring my puzzlement, she invited me inside. The small hall was made smaller by overstuffed bookcases, and plywood boxes filled with firewood. Faded wallpaper on the walls with pictures of roses and dogs. The living room was not much better – more plywood boxes on floorboards and dark rugs with a slumping settee and an armchair. A lampstand with its shade pattern belonging to a century before, more shelves with more books, and ornaments on every dusty surface.

The glowing woman (for this is what she appeared to be doing all the while I was in her presence) asked me if I would care to sit, and would I like a cup of tea.

While she trotted nimbly into the cozy kitchen, I leant over to the side of the armchair and, without thought, picked up a scrapbook from the top of a pile of magazines.

I was feeling distinctly uncomfortable, wondering again

what might have happened to my aunt, waiting for a cup of tea from a distinctive female who, for all I knew, was pouring arsenic into the milk jug. I suspected she possessed a cold and calculating mind, somehow having taken my aunt into her confidence. Had she weaved some devious, convincing story, then murdered Aunt Adeline with poison or some other means – maybe got rid of the home help as well – burying them somewhere within the overgrown bushes in the garden? Then taking over the cottage in this sleepy hamlet, unknown by anyone that two people had been murdered and a cottage stolen?

The more pages of the scrapbook I turned, the more I was convinced Aunt Adeline had been done away with. My suspicions were heightened by reading headlines of some of the cuttings pasted there: "Unidentified benefactor donates £20,000 to local charity" – "Envelope stuffed with money through my letterbox" – "Animal shelter given anonymous donation" and so on. It seems my aunt had money, and lots of it, surely a solid reason to be targeted.

'Looking at my newspaper cuttings, dear one?' the young woman said as she carried a tea tray from the kitchen, back into the living room.

Did this young woman think she could pretend to be an old lady simply by using phrases an older person would use? It was downright creepy.

She placed the tray with its pot of tea and cups onto a small coffee table that stood between us. Then she sat in a graceful manner on the settee opposite. I noticed her stunning eyes, lit with exuberant bright youthfulness yet containing depth not befitting those belonging to someone so young.

'You're part of my family, I know you are, dear one; I can recognize familiar features. I've not lost my faculties yet.'

After speaking this in her melodic tone, she smiled again, a radiant and beautiful smile, showing perfect, snow-white teeth.

I must have stuttered something about my mother. Then those eyes of the angel woman appeared to flash with darker beams of colour. They glared frighteningly, a locked stare as she muttered mother's name, fingers of one hand opening and closing. It was then I noticed a Victorian ring about her wedding finger.

I froze with a mild fright overtaking, half expecting her to leap across the coffee table and throttle me with her refined and delicate hands. Instead, she quickly composed herself and began pouring tea from the silver teapot into one of the bone china cups.

After I replaced the scrapbook onto the top of the magazine pile beside me, she handed over the cup of tea. I took it and held it on my lap. Then she told me more details concerning the scrapbook articles taken from newspapers: how she had won a fortune, and asked her home help to assist in giving money away.

'Much to charities and other worthy causes. Have some as well, I told Belinda, treat yourself and your husband to a holiday, buy a new car even.'

While this stranger sitting opposite was talking with luminous features, I had been sipping my tea without consciously realizing it. I do remember holding my breath, with the sudden shock at the thought that I might drop to the carpet in a poison-induced spasm. But I felt fine, even the beginning of interest for this imposter's tale.

She continued, describing the particular day Belinda had come into the cottage brimming with excitement; how she had found a wonderful holiday including something known only as the ultimate secret.

The enthusiastic Belinda showed her the contents of a thick brochure: a holiday of a lifetime which involved much pampering, being treated as royalty even. It involved travelling on an exclusive yacht to take her to a paradise of an island, one that couldn't be found in any atlas nor able to be seen by satellite. All facilities were there, specifically tailored for the senior citizen. The most sumptuous of chalet suites set in amazing landscaped gardens, incredible arrays of food dishes cooked and prepared from fresh each day. The finest wines and cocktails, fantastic entertainment, even a personal butler on hand to bring into being one's every whim.

Then the ultimate secret, only revealed after a week of blissful holidaying amongst the palm trees and magnificent gardens. Although this would primarily benefit anyone over the age of seventy, Belinda had said, reading from the brochure, ten years or so younger wouldn't rule out being accepted, especially if the price of three million pounds was paid in advance.

The mock aunt leapt to her feet at that point. She explained how sudden exuberant energy often rushed through her, so needing to move, sometimes inspiring her to walk in a balletic fashion, or dance. But after waving those perfectly sculpted arms a few times, she sat upon the settee again.

She declared how uncertain she had been. Surely a waste of so much money spent on a frail lady, the imposter said she had told the home help. But no amount of discouragement could change Belinda's suggestion. Every moment of a luxurious holiday, including the puzzling ultimate secret, was deserved.

The cottage thief told more: how they both travelled by a chauffeur-driven car to a private airport, an executive aeroplane landing somewhere in Spain, and from there, both taken to a port where they boarded the luxury yacht. And after two days aboard they arrived at a small island, miles from any mainland, surrounded by a tranquil sea.

The week's stay in their wooden chalets (made from huge timbers with lofty ceilings) was delightful and restful. Any request, no matter how mundane or ambitious, was fulfilled immediately. Gentle massages, fitness sessions tailored to the older person's body, banquets, dancing exhibitions, carnival and magician acts, guided tours about the enchanting gardens.

I interrupted the mock aunt at that point – I'd learnt enough about the opulence and diversity on the island – I needed to know about the ultimate secret.

'Then I shall tell you, dear one,' the imposter had replied. I'm certain I leant forward in anticipation and, with a trembling hand, placed the cup back onto the tray.

It seems the ultimate secret concerned a spa in a series of connecting underground caverns. Each large domed area over the sparkling water was set with multi-colored lights. The rock walls were decorated with beautiful murals and tapestries. Gentle and soothing music echoed throughout.

The waters of the spa were also lit from underneath, some areas illuminated to give a fair impression of daylight. Under the water were sunken classical statues, girdled with sea flowers; and other sculpted forms, animals and birds, there for those who wished to swim down to study them.

Plenty of bars, cafés and entertainment areas, each one at water level.

'That's not much of a secret,' I recall telling the beautiful identity-stealer.

'Believe it, the secret is much,' she replied. 'You see, dear one, the crystal clear water is rejuvenating. Simply to say, by bathing within, all can regain youthful looks. Wrinkles simply melting away, muscles restored and toned, even bones unbent and refilled, teeth regrown, hair as well. It's a spa of youthfulness – old people made young and beautiful again. And here, dear one, you see the incredible results.'

So this artful woman would have me believe she was a restored Aunt Adeline with the aid of some magical spa on a hidden island. Nothing more than a preposterous tale told by a suspected murderess.

I asked if Belinda had "partaken" of these apparently miraculous waters underground in the caves.

'Oh yes,' that mock aunt told me with an impish grin, 'Belinda went into the spa water the same time as I did.'

'So where is she now?' I asked.

'Still there.'

So Belinda was still in that spa? Why hadn't she come out, to show benefits of shedding years of ageing? My answer was no less than a tirade from the mock aunt, her stunning countenance spoiled by her previously faultless mouth becoming twisted, wide-open eyes, once more fierce. It was as though she had become possessed, this time her fingers moving strangely as if she played an invisible piano. And as she spat out her final words – before I ran out of that humble cottage – Aunt Adeline's old nickname, which my mother had told me, came back into mind: "The spiteful one".

'Belinda, my home help for a good ten years. That's good years, not a good Belinda. A bad Belinda – stealing money from practically the first day she arrived. Did I ever let on I knew? Of course not, I have my pride. It's only money; I could forgive that. Then I won the vast amount of thirty million pounds although she told me I'd won six million.

'I realized her intentions to kill me and take everything I owned, but she had been interrupted by her own plans, the discovery of the island and its ultimate secret.

'It must have been after the third day in that spa. We moved further into the caverns – that's where I led Belinda. Already my legs were stronger, arms gaining more strength for powerful swimming. And finally, there in the deepest spa pool in the final cavern…'

'You drowned her?' I said, mouth dropping open.

'Of course not, dear one. She's still there, swimming in the spa water, not daring to come out. No more to smell freshly cut grass, or sea air, no more to experience true sunshine or the moon's glow.'

'Not getting this,' I said. 'What's stopping her from coming out of the spa, jumping onto the yacht and getting away from the island?'

She gave a strange smile.

'Fright, dear one. I told her a little white lie, that the

ultimate secret wasn't the end – there was a secret to the secret.

'This is how I explained it to that greedy Belinda: that the cave pools were set out in order. On the third day, to obtain full benefit of rejuvenation we needed to swim further into that riddled mountain to the next cavern. Then upon the hour, to the next, and so on. The older ones, still with brittle bones and receding gums and hairline, are in the first spa cavern, the most youthful bathers to be found further in.

'The secret of the secret I told her? Should she swim back to the beginning cavern, she would lose her gained youthfulness. She would go back to her chubby, dry-skinned sixty-year-old self. And more than that, once back at the beginning pool area, she and others would writhe like a pot of worms, racked with pain. To top that, should she come out of the spa waters, she would die in agony even before reaching the entrance.

'So I have much money, still a fortune, even after giving to charities and paying the spa attendants to tell Belinda I had drowned. More than enough to spare to pay for Belinda's stay in the spa pools for at least a year more. She'll never find out what I've done because that's *my* secret.'

ANGELINE

"Reincarnation, fact or fiction?" Patrick read while seated on a plush chair in the hairdressing salon. A shadow, cast across the magazine he held, caused him to glance up.

'Did you say something?' he asked the assistant who stood before him.

She smiled politely and repeated her sentence, 'Ready for your trim now, Mr Snelling,' and continued, 'finished your tea and biscuits? If you'd like to come this way.'

Patrick stood abruptly and knocked a stand holding hair products making the plastic bottles rock on their shelves. A single bell clanged outside from the clock tower in the square, the toll seeming sombre, and deeper than usual.

Jazz music emanated from speakers while he strutted past the sunlit windows after the girl. She showed him to a padded chair facing a mirror, one of many fixed along the magenta walls. His reflection – a darker, more sinister-looking Patrick – stared back at him. Perhaps if this double were able to communicate to the real dimension he might have mouthed the words, "Get out now, before it's too late!"

The assistant switched on spotlights above the mirror while he sat.

'Here's your hairdresser, she'll look after you,' she informed him as another girl walked out from behind the counter by the entrance.

'Mr Snelling? Patrick Snelling from the art college?' the hairdresser asked brightly. She gave a broadly applied grin but with her teeth held together. They glistened within a scarlet mouth, her face partly hidden by curls of brown hair. She adjusted her tinted spectacles.

Patrick was surprised at being recognized by this young woman. He had become forgetful and easily confused after the dreadful car accident. Perhaps his charisma and charm had cast their spell at a gallery or social event, he considered.

'I'm sorry, Miss—'

'Call me Cataline.'

She held up her hands with extended crimson nails adorning each digit, as though proud of those claws, giving evidence to the feline in her name.

'Cataline, I can't remember us meeting. You do seem familiar though. Maybe you studied at evening classes.'

The hairdresser sounded blunt while touching his charcoal-grey locks, 'You don't know me.' Now, with exaggerated gaiety in her voice, she said, 'What masterpiece do you want? I recommend taking it short on the sides,' and she scooped up coils of hair with the edges of her palms, 'keeping length on top. Modern, if you like; trendy, if that's possible.'

She rubbed the top of his head as if petting a dog, one of her nails scratching his skull.

Patrick agreed to the hairstyle. He was led across the varnished stone tiles, passing nine other chairs, each standing in a pool of hair. The suppliers of these locks and tresses sat still with blank expressions, hairdressers trimming and clipping, or preening their hairstyles with foams and sprays.

Patrick sat on a bench at the rear of the salon and positioned himself so that the back of his head was in a basin.

Another assistant who daubed shampoo onto his crown was silent other than to say, 'Take your specs off.'

Patrick enjoyed the sensation of his scalp being massaged while listening to the loud music. The top of his spine ached as the assistant washed his hair, the rim of the basin pressing into the back of his neck, his Adam's apple prominent.

Once the washer had finished her job, Patrick's head was towel-dried and he was shown back to his chair.

A blue gown was held in front of him so that he could pass his arms through holes in it. Then the gown was placed over his chest and tied at the back. A dry towel, put around his neck, was tucked into the back of his collar.

Cataline appeared again and she pulled his spectacles from his hand, saying, 'I'll take those,' before placing them on a shelf. 'Chunky lenses,' she added. 'Your eyeballs are all small and watery, don't mind me mentioning?'

The hairdresser picked up a pair of scissors from a trolley and began to trim his sideburns. Patrick, being extremely short-sighted, could see only Impressionist images in the mirror, with glare from the spotlights bloomed into hazy, glowing spheres.

His head twitched involuntarily.

'Keep still,' Cataline snapped. 'Don't want these scissors cutting your skin, do we. Keen as a razor they are.'

He sucked in his bottom lip like a scolded child might and

let his eyelids drop, to muse on the works of Millais and Rossetti.

At first, Cataline was silent while snipping here, snipping there, pulling his head one way then pushing it the other with a deliberate manner, attentive to her task.

'So does the college still have its history of art course?' she suddenly questioned.

Patrick was broken from his meditation.

'Yes, I'm the head tutor of that department. I really am wondering how you know me.'

Cataline laughed. It was an odd, strangled laugh, as if forced.

'That silly ol' college, looking like a supermarket, plonked on the hill. I watched students trying to reach the top once, after it snowed and the road had gone all slippery. Up they climbed...' *snip*, *snip*, 'and down they slid, with their hands and feet freezing. Quite amusing, really.'

Patrick creased his brow with puzzlement while rubbing his stippled chin. If he had been wearing his spectacles, he might have seen the hairdresser glowering to his reflection. He spoke up.

'You must have some connection with the college.'

'Let's see now,' *snip*, *snip*, *snip*, 'there's Natalie, and Allison,'

'Allison Murray?'

'No, Allison Wingate; big Peter,' *snip*, *snip*, 'and Angeline.'

Upon that name registering, the muscles in Patrick's neck became solid and his torso jerked forward.

'Whoa there, old man,' Cataline cried out, pulling him back by his shoulders. 'I can't style your hair properly if you keep moving around now, can I? Don't you ever listen?' For

Patrick, her abrupt words were washed away with a muddy blend of painful and sweet recollections as tears began to form. She appeared concerned. 'Something upset you? Have a natter; part of the job bending an ear to customers.'

With a sniff, Patrick composed his crumpled features.

'It wasn't anything — well, yes, it was,' he admitted.

Cataline retrieved a stool, placing it beside his chair. After perching her slender form upon it, she put her head near to his, as if she were his confidante.

'Go on, carry on,' she whispered hurriedly.

He began, 'As you seem to know, I teach history of art at the college. Twenty-five years, on and off. And in all that time, amongst the hundreds of students I've taught, there's one I consider to be – to have been – quite extraordinary. Look, I really shouldn't be telling you this.'

Cataline possessed an intent look as she dragged a comb down the back of his cranium with the scissors quickly snipping and producing a fine shower of hair.

'Keep going, I'm interested.'

'Alright, the student in question was called Angeline. And that's as much as I'll say. If you knew Angeline, you know what happened.'

'I don't, Mr Smelling, I mean Snelling. It might not be the same Angeline,' *snip*, *snip*, *snip*. 'Talk about anything you like. I'm used to it, really I am,' *snip*, *snip*, 'anyway, it helps to get stuff off your chest.'

How considerate of this young person to listen, Patrick thought.

'Angeline was blessed with an intriguing mind. Truly charming in manner and appearance, with quite distinctive red hair; patient, kind, not much older than you, I would estimate. In fact, if I had my glasses on, I'd say you bear a remarkable resemblance to her.'

'Steady on,' *snip*, *snip*, *snip*, 'I s'pose that's meant to be a compliment.'

Cataline's breathing was quickening, and rasping in Patrick's ear.

'You're welcome,' he continued. 'Anyway, being such a remarkable student, I started giving lessons after hours. Sometimes Angeline would come to my home during the weekend for me to examine a project, or for her to study my art books and paintings.

'I may be almost fifty – believe it or not – but still, after couple of months she took to me, you could say. I didn't encourage her; she was an intelligent and strong-willed nineteen-year old who knew her own mind. We became more than tutor and student. It happened without warning; it took me quite by surprise.'

Cataline's words were pressing. 'What happened then?'

'Why am I telling you this?'

She pushed his head forward without care so that his chin almost touched his breastbone.

'Because you have to,' she replied.

Patrick knew this answer to be correct. He had not allowed himself to speak with anyone about Angeline until now. It would be an unloading of a burden.

With a guttural and muffled voice, he said, 'We fell in love.'

Cataline sniggered.

'So polite,' *snip*, *snip*, 'fell in bed, you mean.'

She held the scissors upright and closed. Her other hand

grasped Patrick's neck, with her nails making marks on his flesh.

'Well really,' said Patrick, feigning offence. 'Not like that at all. We wanted to share our lives, be together for always. And we would have, had it not been for…we were going to get married, you see. Excuse me.' He moved a finger over his damp eyelids. 'Then the pointless accident.' Cataline's snipping had started again and had become urgent with her hands twitching, and the scissors lungeing at chunks of Patrick's greying hair. He continued, 'I killed her. By accident. How could I have harmed one hair on that precious head?' He paused as if waiting for confirmation. All at once the music seemed even louder and a hair-dryer started its hoarse exhalation two chairs away. Cataline was weeping, and revolving his chair. He said, 'My poor girl, I didn't mean to make you—'

His sentence was cut short when she tore the tinted glasses from her taut face and with her other hand, took hold of her fringe. With a flourish, she pulled the umber wig from her head, waves of flame-coloured tresses flowing out and down from under it.

The tutor stared, wide-eyed and wide-mouthed, as he saw Angeline before him, as alive as he was, and he shouted with astonishment, 'My angel, it's you, you've come back!' and he held out his arms to embrace her.

To avoid him, the hairdresser spun his chair to face the mirror again. She put her luxuriant mane next to his, red against diluted black, as if posing with him for a photograph. Then, brushing her own tears from tinted cheeks with others glistening in her narrowed eyes, she simpered with a peculiar voice, 'Have you missed me? Tell me how much you've been aching for me.'

'This can't be happening, but tell me it is; I've longed for you – like you've longed for me.'

After this declaration, her demeanour changed instantly.

With a hate-filled scowl, she cried out, 'So damned vain; how could you possibly give real love, you doddering old fool!'

'My darling, what are you saying?' Patrick shook his head in consternation. 'How is this possible? The car was a mangled wreck; the tree branch, through the windscreen, into your passenger seat…'

Cataline reached into the back pocket of her jeans and took out sheets of cream paper, and threw them onto his lap. It was as if she sapped his strength. As he dissolved, she became stronger, her voice now firm and demanding.

'Angeline's essay, read it.' He unfolded the papers with shaking hands. 'Go on,' she urged, 'I want to hear it all.'

Patrick gazed longingly to her reflection. He was certain she must be an apparition, expecting her to vanish at any moment as she shivered as if cold or about to dematerialize. He tore his sight away from her to examine the first page of the essay and read in a shuddering voice, 'A study of Van Gogh's self-portraits.'

Angeline had never spoken about her family so how would Patrick know that swaying beside him was Angeline's disturbed twin sister? How to have known that upon the death of her cherished sibling, Cataline's mind had become unhinged?

She had been spying on him for many months, sometimes following him to work and even to his house; blaming him for the loss of her sister. She loathed him and wanted to punish him.

Cataline's delicate face was marred by a manic expression as she snatched up the Van Gogh essay and stuffed it into a pocket. Then, with hissing from pursed lips, she raised her scissors until the sharp blades touched one of Patrick's ears. And with a strange quivering sigh, she cut off his left ear lobe, with a *snip*.

THE BENEFACTOR AND THE GHOST

Lightning appeared as jagged streaks above the sea. And a voice was heard inside of the Smugglers Arms, echoed as though spoken from a distance, 'Do you believe in ghosts?'

Henry Sims was startled. It was difficult for him to locate the source of those words with their melancholic tone and strange reverberations. He looked about the small, beamed room with its abundance of wooden panelling. First to the cast iron fireplace, then through the flickering flame of a candle on his barrel, to one of the room's sides lined with chairs and more barrels. And when lightning lit the sash window panes once more, a grumbling of thunder came from across the bay, and Henry said, 'Who's there? Show yourself at once.'

At the same moment of his demand, he became fully aware of his surroundings as though he had awoken from a tiny place within the back of his skull.

A change in the ambience outside. A street lamp, casting puddles of light across the cobbled street, went out; even distant hissing from the waves became silent.

And there, in an unlit alcove of the snug, a distinct bluish glow could be seen.

Henry called out, 'What the devil?' as the glow pulsed. It took on a stronger outline, appearing to shift in an organic way like some phosphorescent sea creature. And when it formed into the distinct shape of a figure, a chill ran through him. Surely he perceived nothing less than a ghost in the snug of The Smugglers Arms.

To stand and run would seem an unmanly act but he was compelled to get away from that spectre. Yet it held some power over him, draining his strength and sapping any will to move.

By an unknown cue, he heard more echoed phrases spoken clearly and the ghostly apparition took on more substance. Distinct elements could be made out: features on the head, a shirt collar and jacket with sleeves, and hands even, those seeming to be resting on a luminous, open book.

Henry's voice trembled as he asked, 'What do you want of me?'

The words emanating from the ghost continued, now more insistent, 'You can hear me?'

'I can hear you, yes. What have you done? I'm unable to move although I can think clearly but without memory. Are you a spectre sent to bring evil puzzles to warp my mind, to drive me insane? Already I feel…'

'Unreal?'

'Quite the opposite: too real. A waking dream of a high perception that I am certain is about to change into a terrible nightmare. I should flee from your alarming entity if only I could move but my limbs have turned to heavy metal.'

The spectre's voice continued, tinged with excitement.

'So you can see me as well?'

The glow gained strength, showing the ghostly form accentuated like a neon chalk painting.

With Henry's brow creasing with perplexity, he said, 'I see your strange phantom presence more defined by the moment and wonder why you haunt this snug. Is this a personal visitation?'

The ghost voice still echoed, though now stronger and without distortion.

'You could say that.'

'For what reason? I have done nothing wrong; never have I harmed a soul.'

The visitant replied, 'This I know. In fact, the opposite would be true. Much right, helping many. What do you remember?'

'I do believe I have been suffering from amnesia,' Henry answered, his tone, previously edged with worry, suddenly transforming with elation. His mind was opening again like a blossoming flower, senses refreshing as though muffs to his ears were being taken away and blinkers lifting from his eyes. 'Now recalling much – I'm here in the snug of The Smugglers Arms waiting for someone. Yes, I await … I will say no more.'

The spectre now stood in impressive detail as if a real person bathed in a full moon's cold light.

'But you must, for your own good. Although I know the identity of your visitor, as well as the reason for his visit. You have nothing to fear. I'm not hear to judge, turn your mind or worry you. My mission is to help, nothing more. You are a respected benefactor to many; consider me your benefactor.'

The reaction to those words was swift and abrupt.

While Henry nervously stroked his greying beard, he replied with annoyance, 'Why do you call me a benefactor? I know of no such person.'

'But you are known for your help with the poor houses, as well as improving conditions in the mills and factories. Your reticence to take any praise is now well-known. Take that beard off.'

Henry's cheeks reddened with anger.

'It is one thing to be tormented by a ghost but another to be insulted. I have no shaving equipment and even if I had, why should I shave off my beard, for you or anyone else?'

'You know as well as I do,' the spectre continued, 'please, remove it, now. I wish to see your fine features.'

'For what reason?' said Henry but began to remove the false beard all the same. Once he had peeled the beard from his distinguished face, he laid it on the barrel next to his tankard of ale. 'Are you satisfied? I have done as you asked. Now my request — it's time for you to leave, to be swallowed back into the miasmic pit from whence you came. I have been haunted enough. Go back to the past and may you rest in peace rather than your insistent stubbornness to remain on this Earth.'

The volume of Henry's voice had risen to the height of a pulpit-like sermon and, as if his words had taken his strength, he leant forward with his head hanging low.

The blue-illuminated spectre's reply was precise.

'I will tell you this much. I'm not from the past, nor am I in your present. Listen and try to understand. I'm from a time ahead of you.'

Henry was unimpressed and merely snorted.

'Just as I guessed, one of Dickens' ghosts from a Christmas future. Then what are you called, if spirits can still have names.'

'There's no need for you to know. I visit here to tell you something of the utmost importance.'

Henry replied, 'How can I believe a word you say? This could be some demon trick. Already you are becoming bluer and light up even more strangely, there in the corner. Why should I trust you?'

'I know much about your situation. I repeat, I'm here to help. Let me start by asking about the money pouch that was hidden in a secret pocket of your waistcoat. It contained two hundred pounds and five guineas, am I correct?'

Henry stood, swaying, pushing back the captain's chair so that it scraped across the floorboards, and he bellowed, 'No thief will come near, no matter how ingenious their entrapments! I begin to understand; it's becoming as clear as that lightning in the black sky: here we have a Pepper's ghost trick albeit a sophisticated one. Come out of hiding, you smoke and mirror criminal!' But clasping the place near his heart where the money pouch should have been, Henry's previous confidence vanished. 'You insult my intelligence by taunting, after you've stolen from me? What disgusting creature are you?'

The ghost spoke quickly: 'I will endeavour further explanation to our unique situation. Please listen carefully. I am, to you, indeed an apparition – but from your future, 2025 to be exact. I'm able to communicate with the aid of highly sophisticated equipment.

'Before our contact I learnt a lot about you, Henry Sims, respected politician and public speaker, who has a secret not many people are aware of; and those that do know, are sworn to secrecy. You are a benefactor of the highest generosity helping those less fortunate ones. You're here in the snug bar of the Smugglers Arms tonight, having again rented the room from the landlord for your private use only. You were to pass on another magnanimous money gift to Sir Christopher Plumber. He was due to arrive in less than thirty minutes time.

'The money meant for Sir Plumber, for the aid of orphans in London's workhouses, was stolen by the landlord of The Smuggler's Arms.'

Henry said, 'You somehow take the money and then accuse the landlord of doing so? You stoop low, sir.'

'Not so.'

'This is preposterous,' Henry continued, 'The landlord is in the saloon bar, serving customers. I am here talking to a villainous actor involved with an intricate ploy.'

'Of course you wouldn't believe me. You must prove it. Do you see anything in the room, other than myself, appearing to be supernatural or other-wordly?'

Henry glanced over to a rectangle of golden light seen to hover above the floorboards, to the left of the fireplace. 'Now perhaps I do. Seemingly a magical door.'

The spectre spoke clearly.

'Then you must walk through that door. But first, go to a window and look over your shoulder at the reflection. Then you will see the truth.

'At nine thirty-five on a stormy September night in 1879,

a man you trusted, and paid to rent a snug bar in this public house, walked in unexpectedly and after a particularly vicious act of violence, stole the money pouch from your person.' Henry was inspecting his reflection in the darkened panes of the window, seeing a kitchen knife buried up to its hilt in his back. And as a blanket of confusion descended, he staggered towards the door of golden light while the shimmering ghost hunter spoke on. 'The landlord killed you in a terrible act of cowardly, cold blood. Now pass through to heaven, your paradise, to final rest and peace. You see, Henry Sims, I am not the ghost. You are.'

DAISY 8112

As a splash of sunlight lit the interior of the inn, Professor Meredith explained further, 'Daisy 8112, our Artificial Intelligence system, outranks human intelligence. Faster, perfectly logical, intuitive beyond even the finest of minds.'

His friend Norman drank the last of the ale from a pint glass. 'So you have created an incredible computer, programmed with ultimate understanding?'

'Yes, including awareness of self, knowing she's a mind without a body, without nerve endings, who has emotions and unlimited mental resources without physical sensations. But now we have a problem.' Intrigued, Norman nodded to promote an explanation. The professor continued, 'After she became fully sentient yesterday, we initiated Daisy's final initiative program.'

'Which is?'

'Love, in all of its facets. After, other than sounds for three hours, silence.'

'Then?'

The professor was agitated. 'She said "terminate me."'

'And those sounds?'

'Sobbing.'

THE EXTRAORDINARY TALE OF KASSARA

What you are about to read concerns an incredible journal, and how that journal was discovered.

As the owner and senior editor of a small publishing house whose main output is true-life naval dramas, it is rare for me to consider anything outside of this remit. However, the astonishing account written on this journal's pages – no matter how too fantastic it is to be true – was compelling enough for me to extend my personal portfolio by publishing a part of it as a chapbook.

My summer holiday in '65 was in Egypt. I hasten to add that this exotic location bears no relation to the incidents within the entries of the journal. Those refer to its own exotic place: Foyer House Island. It is safe to say this island's name or location cannot be found on any map that I know of. This should underline the fictitious nature of the journal yet I was swayed to believe (or some might say, wanted to believe) that this island exists.

Before I begin in earnest, I feel I must describe a peculiar incident. My travels from London to Aegina, by train and ships, was uneventful. After a short stopover on the Greek island, I caught a ferry, sailing to the Egyptian mainland. The crossing was dreadful and a little frightening. A soup of a fog descended half-way and the sea was as rough as could be, for longer than I cared for. When we finally docked I was only too pleased to see, from my vantage point on the open deck, the railed gangplank placed below. While making my way to it as fast as I was able, I saw the deck empty of other people; and there were no other passengers making their way out of the hatches. And while crossing over those planks to solid land, with a glance behind, I noticed no one else disembarking.

I travelled from the port at Alexandria to Faiyum, a busy and bustling town situated not far from the tip of the Red Sea. Settling in at the Hotel Akiiki, I enjoyed the generous hospitality within for two days. The sun's strength kept me indoors and away from their open roof arcades.

The sun on the third afternoon was blisteringly hot. Hiding from its rays within the comfort of air-conditioned rooms for so long, the decision was made to investigate beyond my confines. And so with straw hat firmly in place and clothing loosened I ventured out. I chose to ignore my guide book and simply followed my feet, soon enamoured by the unconventional streets and byways with their mosques and colourful bazaars.

I discovered a quaint café not far from the canal, and sat at a table outside, under a canopy, with the added shade of a coconut palm's fronds. And after ordering an iced mint tea, I watched the men and women in flowing gowns passing by their flat-roofed houses and shops. Then I took out of my pocket a copy of A History of the Dhow, intending to read it until teatime.

A swarthy man on the next table caught my eye; his turning of the head to enable him to read the title of my book was faintly amusing if not a little uncivilized. I tilted the cover to him so he might read it whereupon he nodded.

He explained, in what could be described as a continental accent, his interest of "all things seaworthy" and upon my lighthearted remark of "including dhows?" he stood and walked over to my table. His face did not break the amiable grin and bright eyes he owned. He told me his name was Eduardo Simion – an immigrant from Portugal – and that he was curator at the Sea Museum in Korba Street. I admitted not seeing any such place mentioned in the guides.

He appeared trustworthy and the day was slow and still too hot, so I readily agreed to follow him there in the hope of finding some form of cooling system.

Passing through the loud market, harangued by stallholders with the promise of haggling over a miniature of a tomb, sacred cat or some other trinket, I found it difficult to keep pace with my newly found colleague. He deftly wove his way through the crowded market aisles, waving at insistent sellers as if swatting flies. I did have the opportunity to catch up when he stopped by a stall selling fruit. After purchasing two lemons, he trotted nimbly on, looking back to me to check I still followed.

The side alley was no cooler despite being in shadow. At the end stood a whitewashed building with double doors peeling paint, and an enamelled sign marked "The Sea Museum".

Mr Simion turned a key in the lock and we entered. Once

inside, I realized that two dwellings had been knocked into one but which still made for the smallest of museums.

But interesting exhibits to be found there, all the same. There was a boat similar to a coracle alongside the keel of an old oaken falluca. A row of roughly cut and gaudily painted figureheads seemed to watch me passing by. As he proudly showed me a cannon, my attention was drawn to a raft, approximately six feet square, that had been unceremoniously leant on a wall in a dark corner.

The main platform of the raft was built from lashed lengths of rough timber, still some limpets glued to them. In the middle of it was a circular hole cut and as I wandered over in curiosity, I saw an upturned glass plate there, which I guessed was for viewing underwater.

Underneath, surrounding this plate, were large flagons secured with furred green rope taken through holes of wooden battens. The flagons might once of contained olive oil or vinegar. My acquaintance saw my interest in this peculiar raft and so explained its origin. The structure was found drifting in the Red Sea thirty miles out from the coast of El Quseir, and was brought home and donated to the museum by a friend.

Then my eye was caught by a dead crab incarcerated in one of those flagons. I bent down to inspect it more closely: behind it seemed to be sheaves of paper. I mentioned this to Mr Simion who simply shrugged, and we walked on without any more said about the find.

After I had visited the first floor, seeing rope arrangements, a full mizzenmast appearing from a hole in the floor and other nautical items of passing interest, I thanked my host and bade him farewell.

I was pleased to find the next afternoon cooler than the previous day; some cloud cover made the air heavier but still it was bearable. I sat inside the Cafe Al Omda, partaking of a hookah (one must indulge in another's culture when given the chance). Upon returning to the mint tea, the glass to my lips, an excited Eduardo Simion hurried through the doorway, a look of consternation about his features which changed to a broad smile upon seeing me in my corner.

It seemed that the contents of the flagon were one hundred or so tightly-written pages on rough, handmade paper.

Mr Simion told me that not only was it a remarkable journal but that it was written in English. He had hold of at least fifteen of the pages for me to investigate.

After a brief discussion, it was agreed I copy them word for word, as I am a native English-speaker and so would understand better, and be able to translate any lettering which might have become smudged or obliterated by seawater. Mr Simion said he was busy elsewhere and had to go; although I left the café with him I returned not long after with a fountain pen and notebook in hand. Then, after an initial study of the papers, I found them to be in the wrong order with some of the pages missing, as if they were taken at random from throughout the folio.

So, surrounded by wise-eyed hookah smokers and casual mint tea drinkers, I set about the task of sorting the leaves before copying the words, as read from those pages of the journal, into my notebook.

•••••

Page 1
29th of September, 1895
My name is Anthony Bridgewater. I am writing this whilst looking out to sea, sitting on hot sand with my back to a rock. There is a mechanical man to my left who holds a baton in readiness to conduct his small orchestra. They sit on a stage made from riven slate. They have their backs to a semi-circle of sculpted stones which hide them from the sweeping waves. The conductor has a benign look of anticipation about his lips with eyes wide, and thick, grey eyebrows raised. His frozen countenance and figure is no surprise to me now.

Not far from where I sit is a small cave – protected by boulders – one of many worming through this gigantic pile of rock which is called Foyer House Island. Inside it is a raft I made that will not only be my means of escape, but afford a protection to this journal should I not get back home.

Page numbers unknown
...night I had another peculiar dream. I can report that since being on this island, all of my dreams have been of this lucid kind, seeming to uncover layers of reality previously unknown.

I am on a raft made of green and yellow bottles, staring down into the depths of the ocean where clouds of beautiful fish swim within the sapphire waters. I know exactly where I am: the spot where my ship had foundered. A sun shining like the moon, spreading greenish fingers of light across the dappling waters. Ahead I see the beach holding a row of rocks and these are like massive gnarled knuckles. As the raft drifts to the right on a gentle current, Kassara as the conductor comes into view. Lifting the baton with even more certitude, there a pause as he looks to his audience; whereupon the first upward stroke of this musical wand starts the musicians into a collective wonderment of sound. I have never heard such extraordinary music before – as the violins swell and the flutes glide, a sense of awe and excitement fills my soul. I wish to dive into the clear waters and swim to shore, and then over to Kassara and his wonderful ensemble of musicians.

My wonderment does not stop there; for as my eyes encompass the island, each side of that mountain covered abundantly in trees became brown locks of hair; and Kassara falls prostrate onto the slab which is his pedestal. As though this is a signal, bright and flashing fish dart around and about with seaweed wavering and they form the letters of the name "Kassara". A flock of birds descend to stand on jutting rocks of the mountain. I recognise them to be falcons. They rearrange themselves, and their group becomes an eye with a vivid, green iris. Trees bend and nod over them before becoming upright again; they have acted as an eyelid, giving the appearance of that massive hypnotic eye winking at me.

Pages 5 to 8

...eventuality dawned all at once. Faced with a difficult decision, I put it to the back of my mind so that I might not drag down my spirit, already curling in panic.

Should I swim towards that strange mannequin almost masked by the rock, shaped like a cockle shell, possibly some cultish icon worshipped by the inhabitants of this dismal island?

The men (dressed in their peculiar choices of attire) were barking orders but the actual meanings were lost to the hectic waves and wind. They were hauling the drowned men from the sea, laying them side by side on the sand of the beach. One of the band was searching their pockets.

I dared not swim to the shore to meet them. I am a strong swimmer and despite the waves pummelling me I decided my best course of action would be to dive underwater and head towards a sheltered cove to provide me with cover.

Without warning – a moment after I had raised my eyes to those dreadful, dark clouds – I was sucked into a whirlpool and dragged under.

I was carried along and upwards through a tunnel of rock, freezing black water rushing along with me. I lashed out to hanks of seaweed in an attempt to slow my progress. I knew I was about to be killed, surely thrown with a force against a cave wall at the end. I would be as the crew and passengers of The Galliard: bloated, floating dead and pushed wherever, food for sharks. But some sort of guiding spirit was with me. This tunnel of rock was like a huge oesophagus, drawing water in an out as a living creature would to draw air in and out of its lungs. When I had surfaced in a cave at the end of the tunnel, the moment the direction of those tons of water turned I cradled a stony outcrop with all my strength and pulled myself up onto it. And as the water receded, I climbed as high up the interior rock-face as I was able, slipping on green slime. There was a hole above like a jagged silver disc and the higher I climbed, the more of the sky showed through.

I heard the breathing water surging in and out as I climbed

to the top. I came out, exhausted and shivering, onto a flat rock at the edge of the coast, overlooking those crashing waves. The mountain stood over me, dark and mysterious, wreathes of fog about its summit. There was a path of sorts which I followed; it took me along the edge and around, so that I was closer to the beach that was infested with those brigands or pirates, whatever they were. One of them was wheeling a barrow close to the line of bodies. Others were daring the lashing wind and rain by swimming out to collect wood and other flotsam from the sea. Still another had tied a rope about a tea crate so as to tow it to shore.

Page 10

...imposing figure, taller than the rest, wearing a terracotta jumper and tights with some sort of skirt around his waist, yellow and white. A black patch completely covered one of his eyes. He held a rod and was tapping it upon the rock formation immediately behind the corpses. To my surprise, a large plate of rock slid away, revealing an entrance to a secret cave. They would surely be taking the dead men inside of it to search them at their leisure. These parasites were making me angry and ill, and more so when I recognized one of the victims dragged from the sea to be Mr Roper, my colleague and friend. If I could have leapt at them then as a jaguar might from a tree I surely would have done. Though all I could do was watch but quickly turn away in disgust at their antics.

Page 13

...noticed, twenty feet below, heart-shaped piles of jet-black rocks. From this side of them I stared at the dummy's head covered with fine white hair, arms raised with one hand holding what looked to be a conductor's baton. And more figures before him as still as a tableau made of stone. Behind stood the curve of stones which screened them from the crashing waves.

I decided to head on, with that constant rain adding to my already soaked clothes. Above, the mountain looming out of the dark clouds. I weaved my way through trees and bushes, still feeling a deep sadness at those dead ones, now at the mercy of the body-snatchers. The actions of the strangers on this abysmal island was too terrible to countenance; not amounting to murder but nonetheless despicable.

What if some of the men, seemingly drowned, were capable of resuscitation? I started to run. If I could make my way back down to the shoreline without being seen and somehow open that secret door, then I might be able to save some of my fellows.

I marched in earnest, prepared to fight any of the brigands who would stop me. The rained was slowing. I was suddenly lighter in spirit and changed my mind again; I would need to be cautious of these…

Page 16

As they disappeared through the impressive rock arch into the next bay, I looked down to my right to see the immobile figure on the shore and, from this direction of view, I could see his orchestra. They too sat in eager anticipation of their conductor starting the recital, from what signal I have no idea.

So strange was this, I decided that I must see more closely the unusual arrangement of models by the sea.

The closer I got to them, the more I felt afraid, and a total confusion enveloped me. They looked real people yet frozen as if time had stopped for them all.

Page 47

...raised voices and decided that to hide for the while would be the best option; looking through the low branches of a tree with my body hidden behind its gnarled trunk. What I saw was shocking to the core. There, in sharp, clear daylight, were some of the crew members of The Galliard. My breath seemed to leave my body with the revelation of it. I was compelled to call out to them but before I did, their charismatic leader spoke. His words were difficult to catch; but as much as reached my ears, I have to say it was quite the most extraordinary voice I have ever heard. I am not ashamed to mention, with its unique baritone richness and subtle timbres, my heart lurched with a sort of ecstasy. Some of the others were animated in a peculiar way while more dropped to their knees, there to stretch out prostrate before him as if in worship.

I swear there was some force from that mysterious one, as if he was making the tree invisible, or be made of glass. The impressive frame of Kassara moved...

Page 49

...was Mr Roper, as alive as ever.

How had he released his lungs of salt water and come back to life? How was that possible? I admit that I shed a tear then, so happy to see him unharmed. I wanted to call out to him – "Mr Roper! Mr Roper!" – even run over and fling my arms about the man to hug him like a brother.

But then something had me narrowing my eyes. Not everything was as it should be: he started to walk away and I noticed his gait was different than was usual. We learn small details about our acquaintances and friends without realizing; I must have registered into my brains the manner in which Mr Roper walked. His was always a sloppy gait, I suppose, giving a friendly air to his person. Yet this imposter – surely – was walking differently, almost mechanically.

I would need to keep my mouth sealed, I told myself; as well as my footsteps light. I decided to follow him.

Page 62

...since discovered many more of these mechanical creatures across the island; or rather around its perimeter, some close to the water's edge, others hidden in lagoons and forests of palms while others seeming to hug the mountainside.

What incredible contraptions they are. One day I will dare to sully one of those wondrous creations by opening it up, to discover the intricacies which fit inside. Surely there are cleverly balanced, clockwork mechanisms with rods and gears and pulleys, somehow in perfect concert with electricity in a pure form, and cogs with the finest of teeth.

What I find puzzling is how varied these mechanical creatures are. There were the figures in Turkish garb and black turbans in the wooded area not far from the settlement; an Indian aesthete dressed in fine muslin and gold ornaments; a group of Chinese...

Page 74

...mind reeled at the sight: a mighty pyramid, at least as tall as the largest which stands at Giza. It towered high, lit by many flickering torches along each of its stepped rows. Impressive and huge yet still it was dwarfed by the cavernous space that contained it, the inside of that mountain having been somehow hollowed out.

The floor beneath my feet was made of polished granite squares with grid lines made of crystal. This beautiful material caught the glowing from those torches and seemed to pulsate with their own light.

It took me a good ten minutes to walk the perimeter of the magnificent structure, my attention drawn to the many intricate sets of hieroglyphs expertly incised into the insides of the mountain and highlighted with paint. And there, a huge doorway carved and inset either side with statues dominated one end. My knowledge of Egyptian gods is limited but as I studied them I could see…

Page 95

…incredible if it were true. I began to comprehend: these semi-opaque vessels somehow contained and protected the spirits – the souls even – of those who had drowned. Souls from the Far East, Asia and the Americas; from anywhere, anyone unlucky enough to have been aboard a ship destined to be sunk by those cruel rocks hidden and lying in wait in the ocean.

What type of arcane knowledge had to be acquired even to consider the idea of this? How could it be made to work? The concept owed too much to the imagination.

Nevertheless, there was some kind of proof: did I not see the decomposing body and face of Mr Roper before being wrapped in bandages and ceremoniously burned with others? A week after, Mr Roper, as alive as I am, walking and talking on the bluff?

The indescribable powers which Kassara must have within his control; the limitless genius to create mechanical men and women that moved and seem to breathe like any human being; the unknown processes he was familiar with to somehow install a soul into each of these mechanical creations; breathing life into them, so that they became the dead ones, alive again. And the extreme artistic creativity involved: the faces of the clockwork people matching precisely as if their twin, bearing no difference with the faces of their intended recipients, perfect in…

•••••

I had at that moment finished transcribing the last of the pages given to me by Eduardo Simion when he came into the café at speed, as though someone might be after him. A possibility, I did think at the time, with the way his squarish head swung from left to right, his features full of suspicion.

Catching sight of me at my table at the back, he hurried over. He was a different man to the one I had met earlier in the day. Those eyes of his were coal-black, and I saw then not holding suspicion, but more like fear. Without a word, he contorted his mouth and snatched up the pages from the tablecloth, knocking the oil lamp as he did. He spun fast on his heels and literally ran to the café door. I have not met him again since that day.

The shock I felt was deep; there was a certain unrealness about his actions, even more than those tales told in the journal pages.

I think I must have sat there for a while as though put into a trance. It took a good ten minutes of rumination to come to terms with the unexpected insult – because that was what it felt like – finally rising from my chair so as to go pay the bill.

The café interior was relatively dark compared to the slab of sunlight the other end. There were candles at the back, in tapped brass containers, murky and smokey shadows and blacked-out alcoves. Before I moved away, my attention was drawn to a man in a previously darkened corner: a flare of a match and the lighting of a beeswax candle before him chased those shadows away. He must have been lingering in that darkness over a cup of black coffee on the wooden table before him.

I swear an oath of truth here: he was dressed in a dark burnt-orange sweater, and had a long beard plaited with ribbon. I caught sight of a yellow and white skirt, and one of his strong calves covered with terracotta-coloured stockings. He seemed larger than life, cutting out the space there which seemed to be vibrating all about him. Then, while pushing some brown locks from his forehead, with one eye socket showing only a bone bowl, the other containing a penetrating green eye, he winked at me.

Peter Carmel, Faiyum, August 1965

If you enjoyed reading Two Dogs At The One Dog Inn And Other Stories please consider leaving a review on Amazon – thank you.
Also available as a Kindle ebook.

David John Griffin is a writer, graphic designer and app designer, and lives in a small town by the Thames in Kent, UK with his wife Susan, and two dogs called Bullseye and Jimbo. He is currently working on the final draft of his fifth novel.

His first novel, *The Unusual Possession of Alastair Stubb*, was published by Urbane Publishing in November 2015. Urbane also published David's literary/psychological novel entitled *Infinite Rooms*. His book called *Abbie and the Portal* (a science fiction time travel adventure) was published in 2018. The urban fantasy novel *Turquoise Traveller* was published in 2019. One of his short stories was shortlisted for The HG Wells Short Story competition in 2012 and published in an anthology. He has several other stories published in various collections.

You can find out more about David at
www.davidjohngriffin.com

Also available on Amazon:

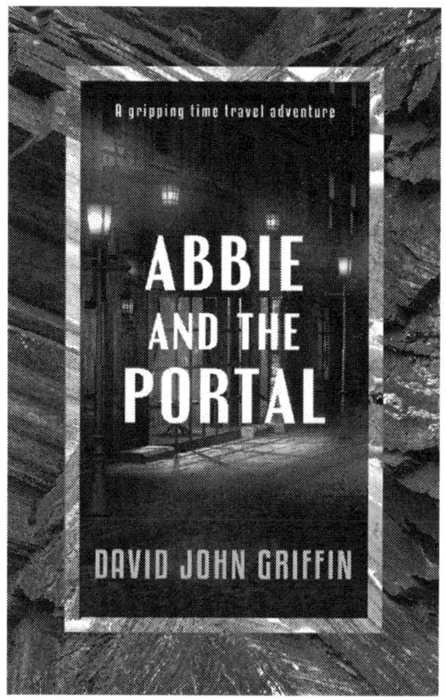

ABBIE AND THE PORTAL

"Help me, I'm trapped" is the plea from a young woman named Abbie Concordia, written as a mysterious note found inside a Victorian book called Caving in Faringham. Terry Bridge, a reporter for The Charington Echo, takes up the challenge to save her...from the past. A gripping sci-fi time travel adventure story that will captivate you from beginning to end.

"Great premise, scintillating pace, and a most intriguing plot"
"Utterly absorbing"
"A story that had me engrossed from the start"

Printed in Great Britain
by Amazon